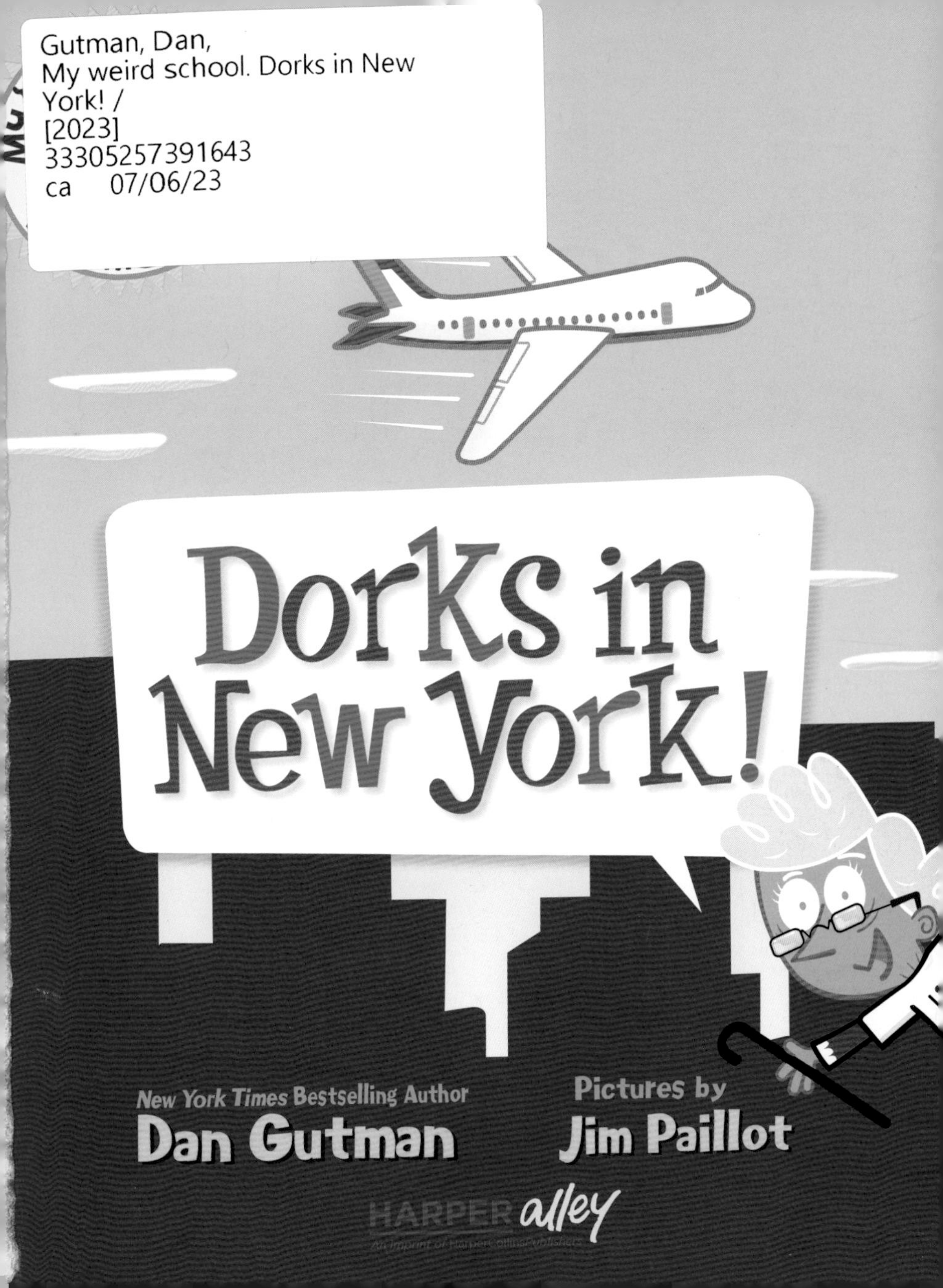
Dorks in New York!
New York Times Bestselling Author
Dan Gutman
Pictures by
Jim Paillot
HARPER alley
An imprint of HarperCollinsPublishers

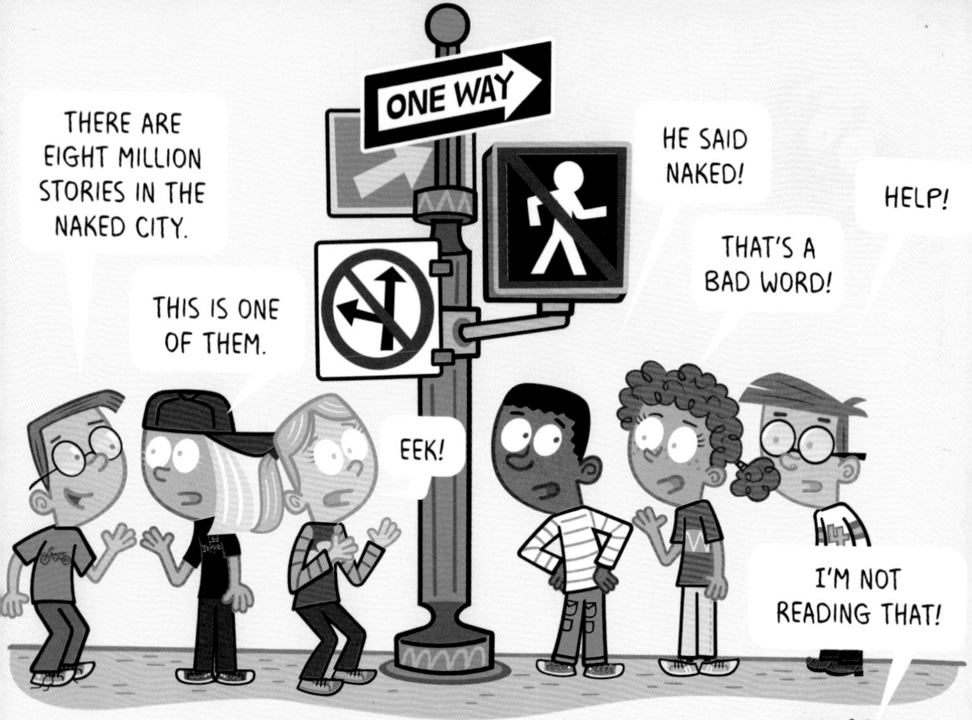
ONE WAY
THERE ARE EIGHT MILLION STORIES IN THE NAKED CITY.
THIS IS ONE OF THEM.
EEK!
HE SAID NAKED!
THAT'S A BAD WORD!
HELP!
I'M NOT READING THAT!

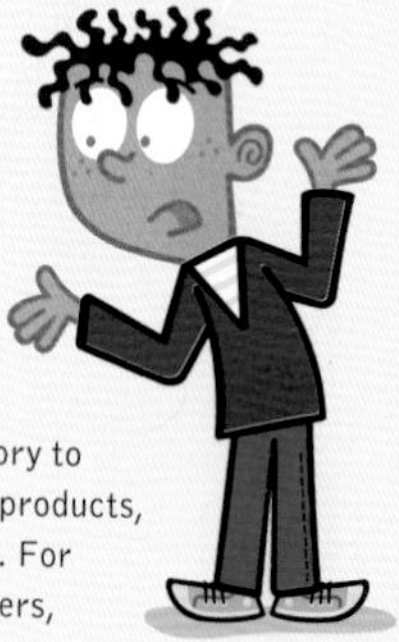

HarperAlley is an imprint of HarperCollins Publishers.
My Weird School Graphic Novel: Dorks in New York!

For information address HarperCollins Children's Books, a division of HarperCollins Publishers, 195 Broadway, New York, NY 10007.
www.harperalley.com

Library of Congress Control Number: 2022935789
ISBN 978-0-06-322971-6 (pbk. bdg.) — ISBN 978-0-06-322972-3 (hardcover bdg.)

Typography by Martha Maynard
22 23 24 25 26 RTLO 10 9 8 7 6 5 4 3 2 1
❖
First Edition

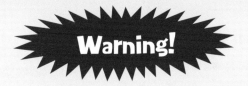

Warning!

THIS BOOK CONTAINS SCENES OF GRAPHIC VIOLINS, AS WELL AS CAR CRASHES, WILD RAMPAGING ANIMALS, THROWING THINGS OFF TALL BUILDINGS, ROBBERY, DUMB STUNTS, PEOPLE FALLING INTO OPEN MANHOLES, GROWN-UPS BEHAVING VERY POORLY, OBNOXIOUS CHILDREN, THE TOTAL DESTRUCTION OF PRICELESS OBJECTS, DISTORTED HISTORY, BAD JOKES, SWORD FIGHTING, IMPLAUSIBLE SITUATIONS, AND PEOPLE WALKING INTO DOORS.

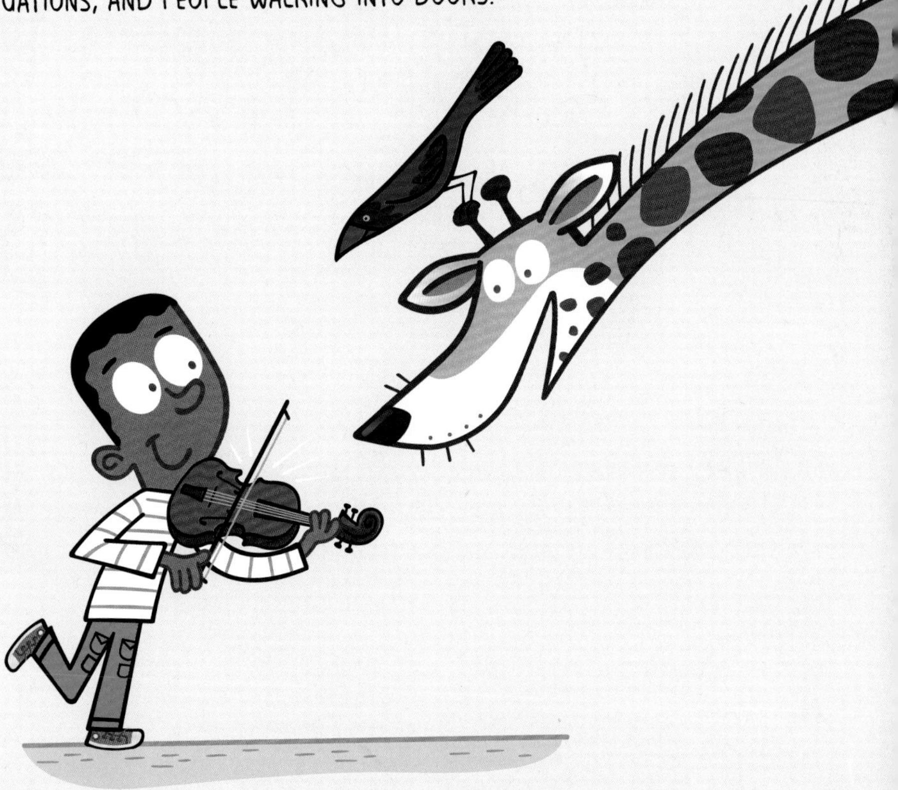

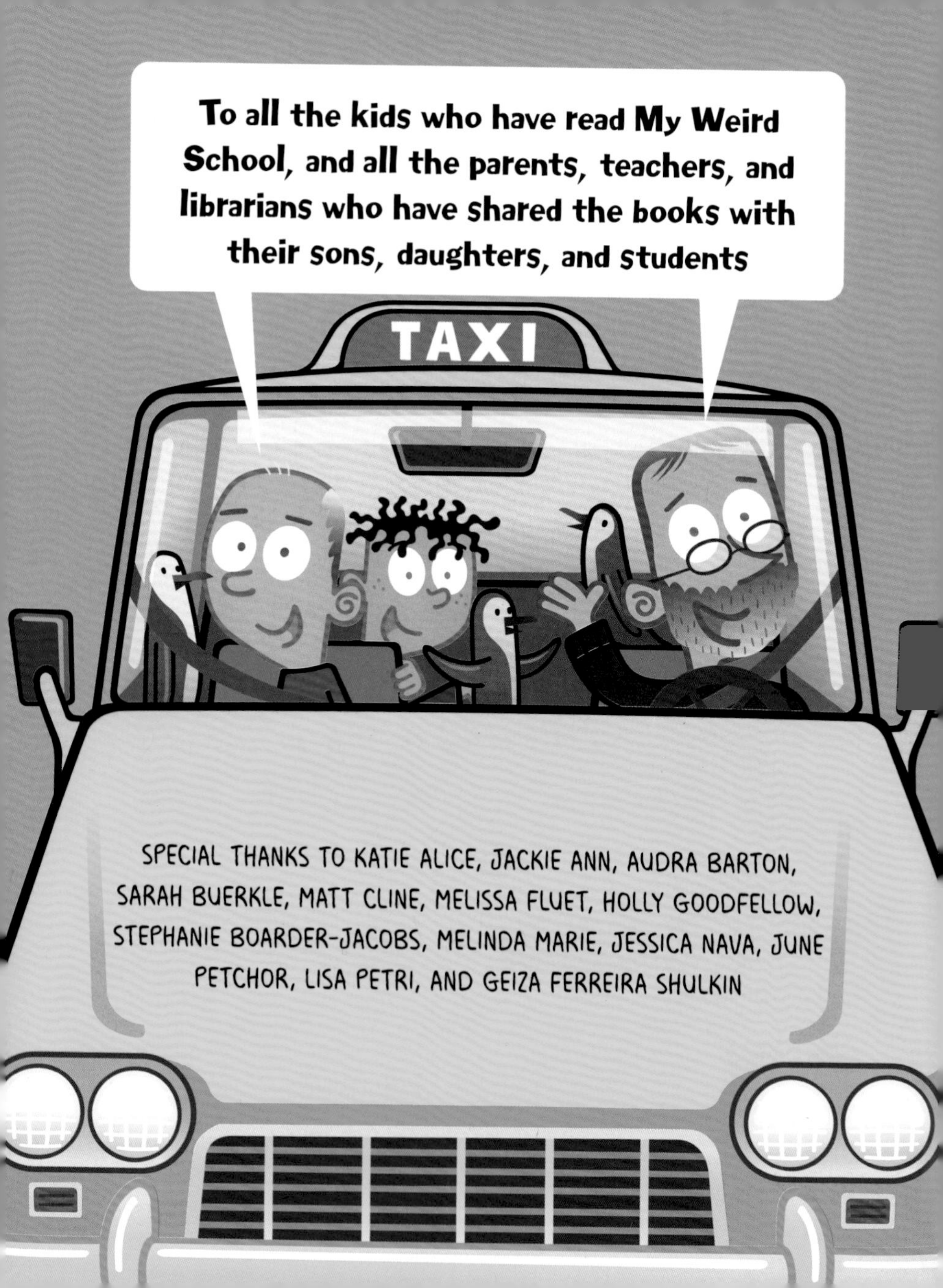
To all the kids who have read My Weird School, and all the parents, teachers, and librarians who have shared the books with their sons, daughters, and students
TAXI
SPECIAL THANKS TO KATIE ALICE, JACKIE ANN, AUDRA BARTON, SARAH BUERKLE, MATT CLINE, MELISSA FLUET, HOLLY GOODFELLOW, STEPHANIE BOARDER-JACOBS, MELINDA MARIE, JESSICA NAVA, JUNE PETCHOR, LISA PETRI, AND GEIZA FERREIRA SHULKIN

Table of Dis-Contents

THAT STUFF DRIVES ME CRAZY!

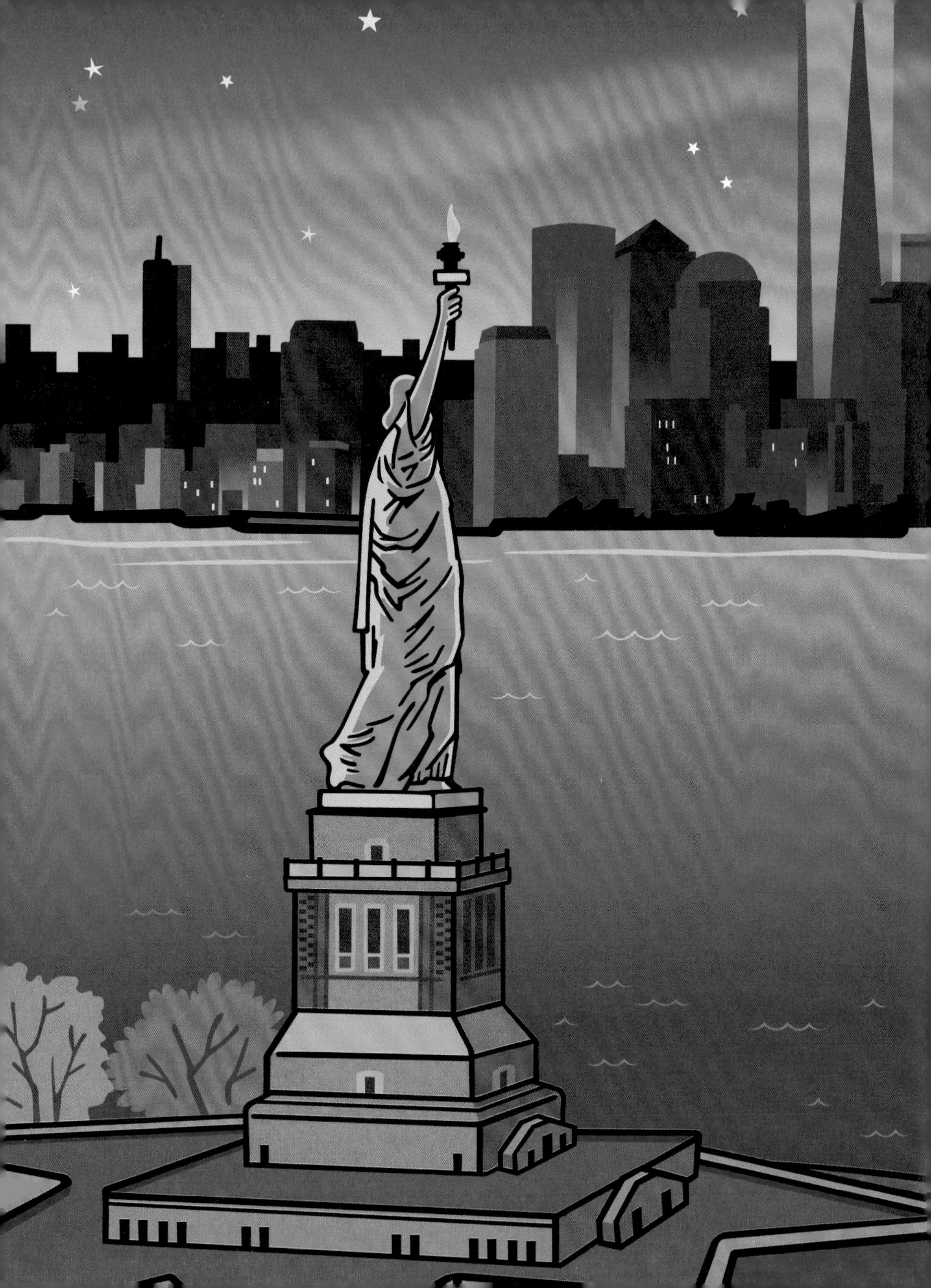

CHAPTER 1

People Who Leave Their Shopping Carts in the Middle of the Parking Lot

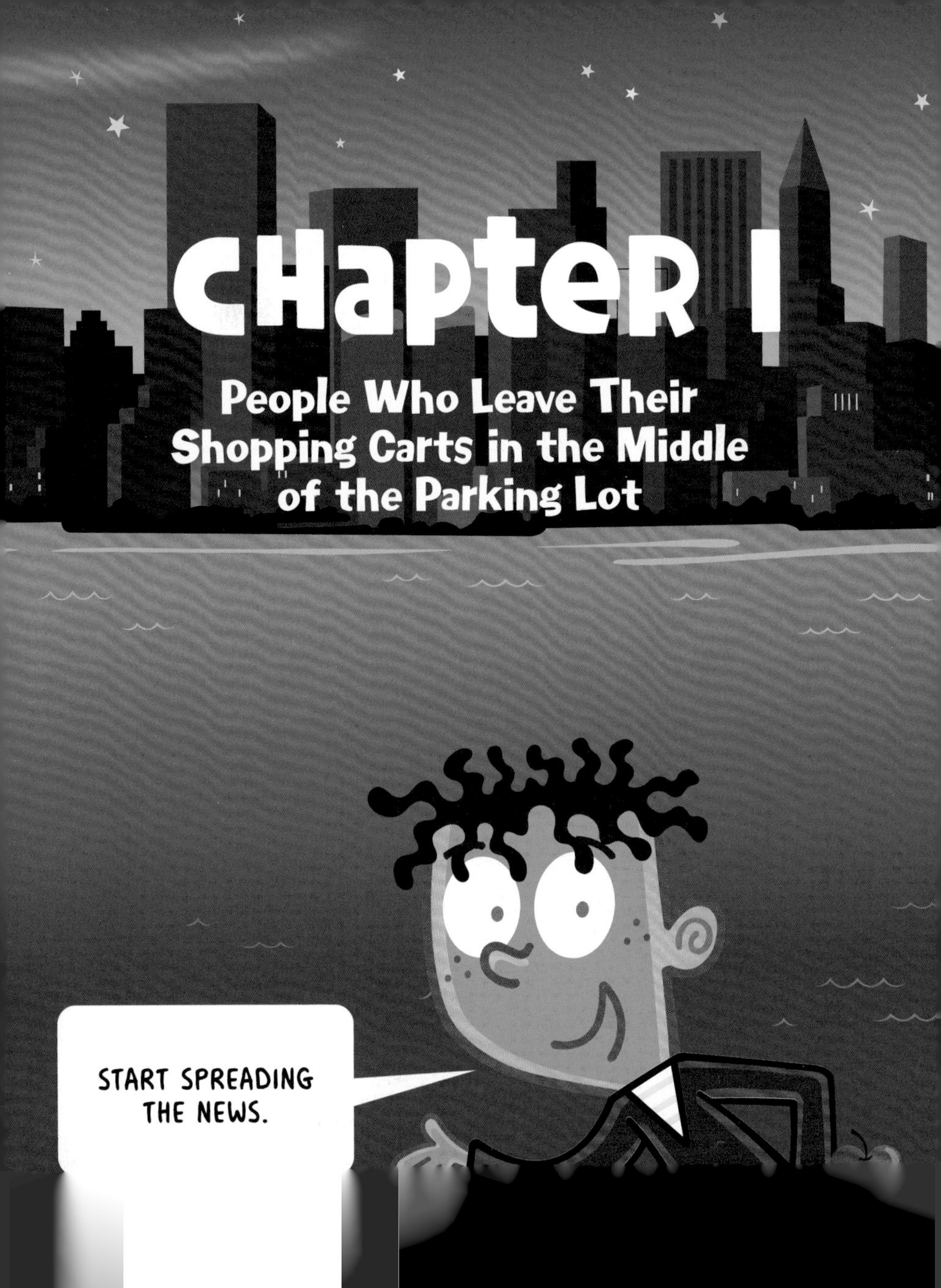
START SPREADING THE NEWS.

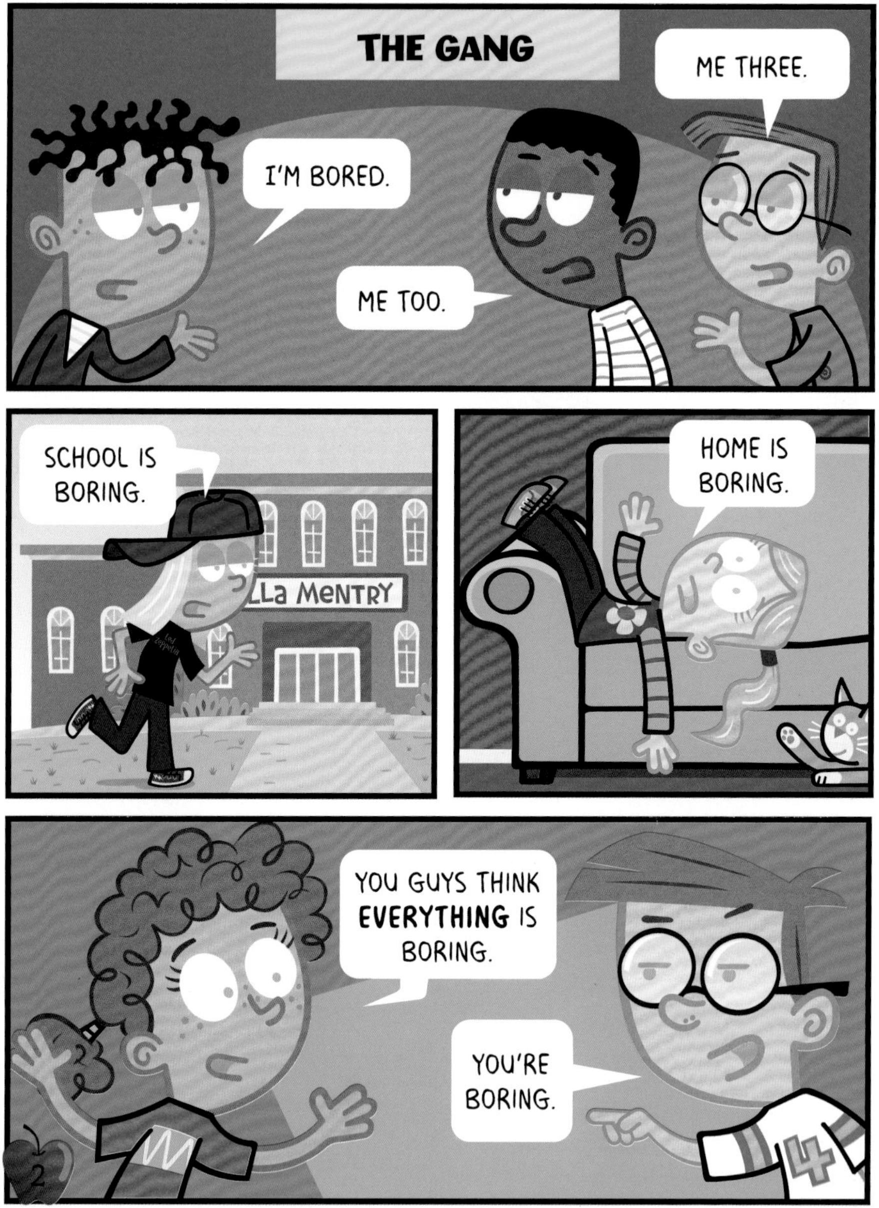
THE GANG
I'M BORED.
ME TOO.
ME THREE.
SCHOOL IS BORING.
LLa MeNTRY
HOME IS BORING.
YOU GUYS THINK **EVERYTHING** IS BORING.
YOU'RE BORING.

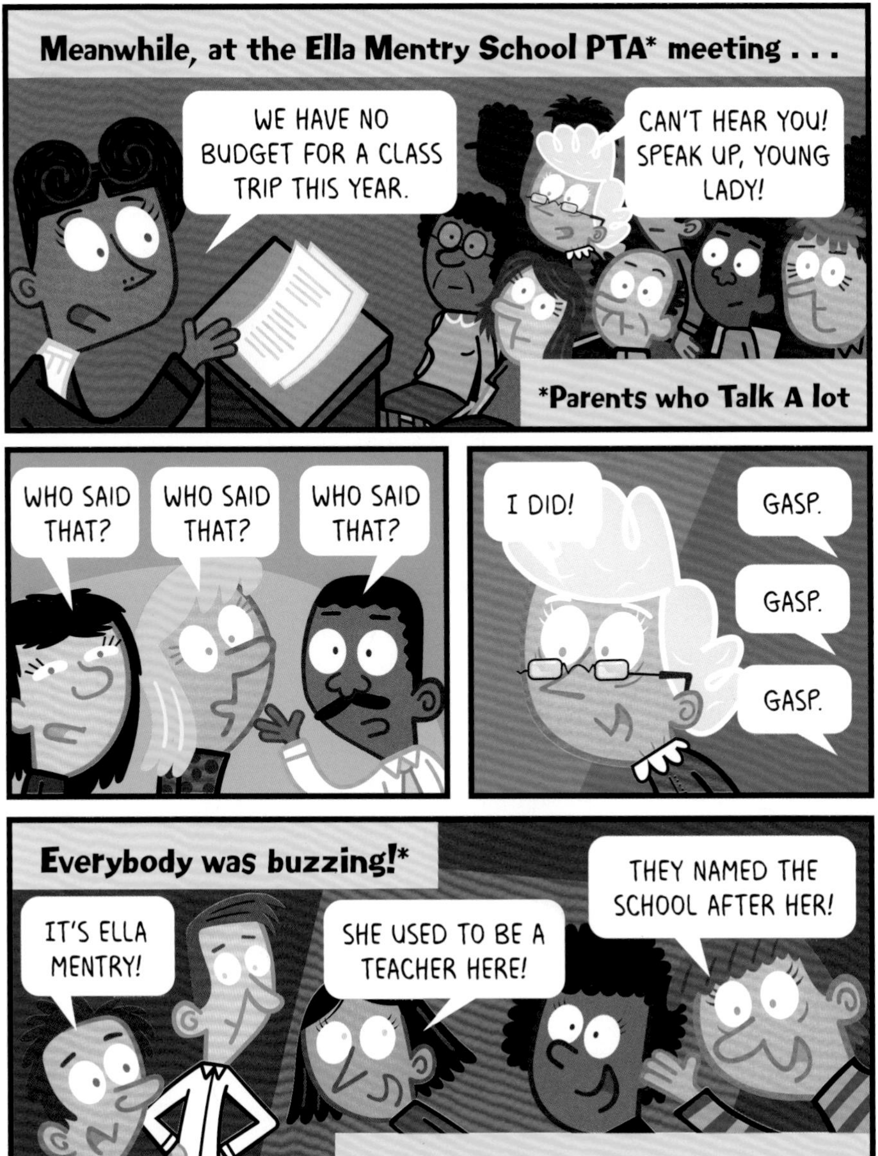
Meanwhile, at the Ella Mentry School PTA* meeting . . .
WE HAVE NO BUDGET FOR A CLASS TRIP THIS YEAR.
CAN'T HEAR YOU! SPEAK UP, YOUNG LADY!
*Parents who Talk A lot
WHO SAID THAT?
WHO SAID THAT?
WHO SAID THAT?
I DID!
GASP.
GASP.
GASP.
Everybody was buzzing!*
IT'S ELLA MENTRY!
SHE USED TO BE A TEACHER HERE!
THEY NAMED THE SCHOOL AFTER HER!
*But not like bees; that would be weird.

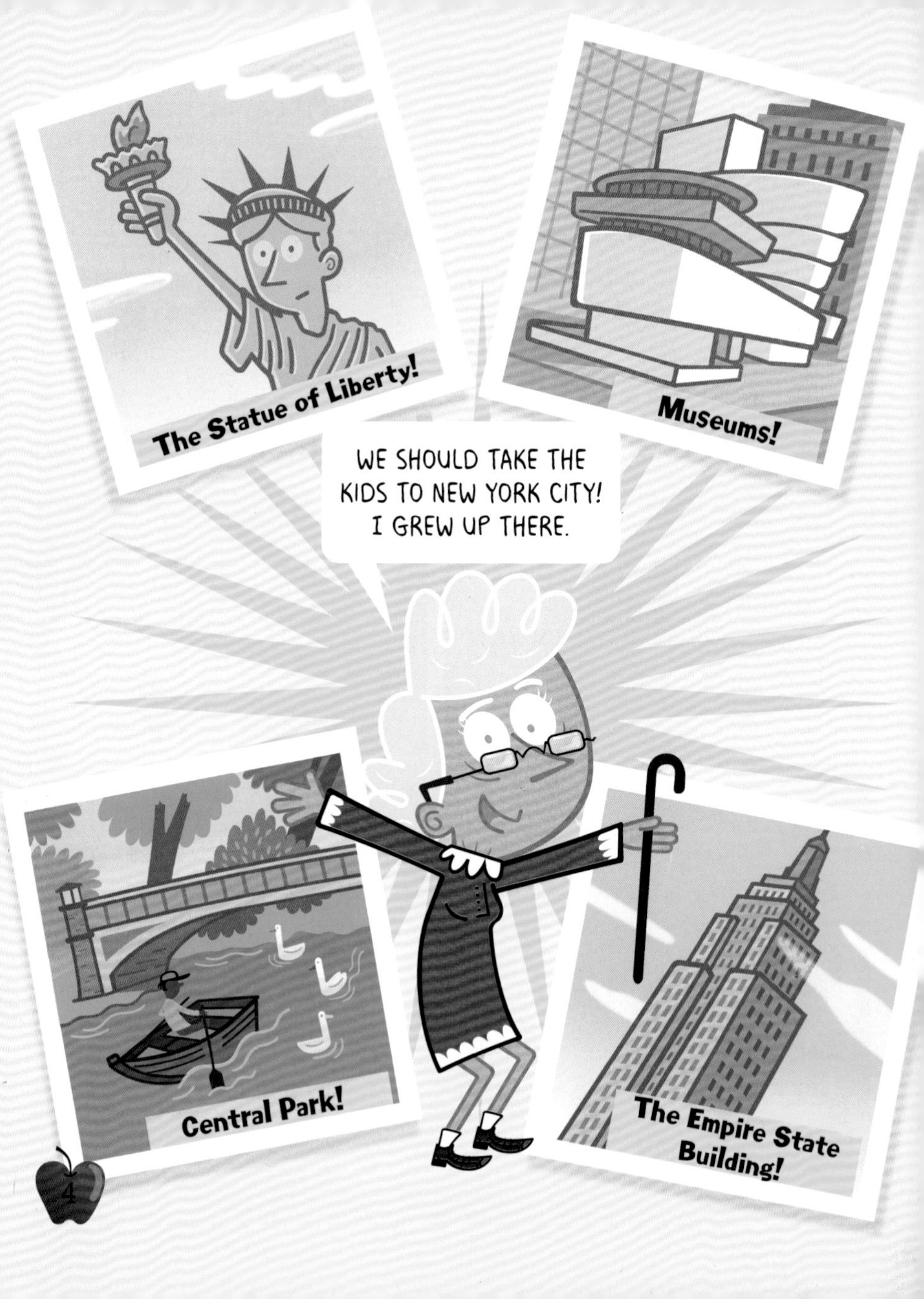
The Statue of Liberty!
Museums!
WE SHOULD TAKE THE KIDS TO NEW YORK CITY! I GREW UP THERE.
Central Park!
The Empire State Building!

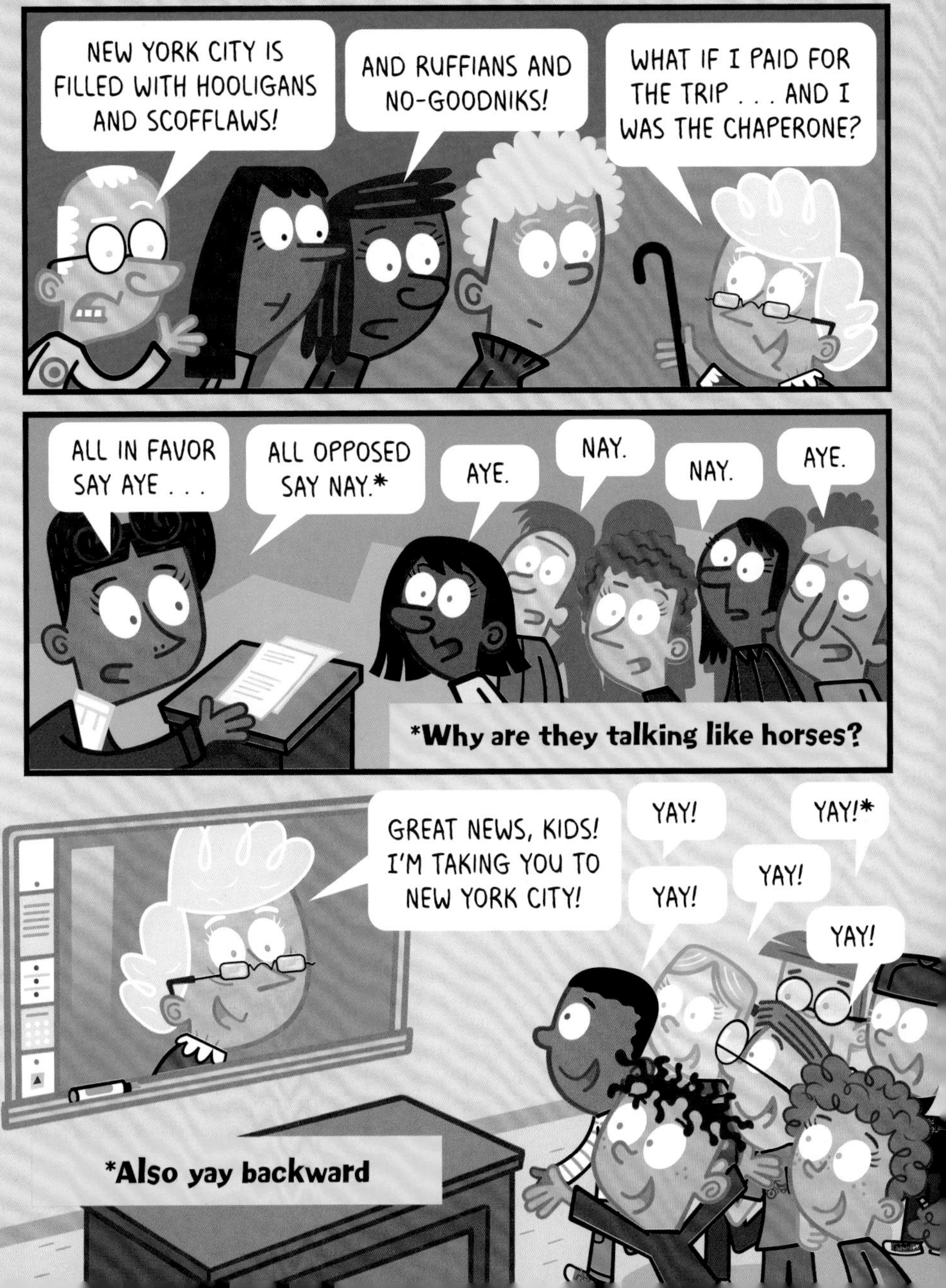
NEW YORK CITY IS FILLED WITH HOOLIGANS AND SCOFFLAWS!
AND RUFFIANS AND NO-GOODNIKS!
WHAT IF I PAID FOR THE TRIP . . . AND I WAS THE CHAPERONE?
ALL IN FAVOR SAY AYE . . .
ALL OPPOSED SAY NAY.*
AYE.
NAY.
NAY.
AYE.
*Why are they talking like horses?
GREAT NEWS, KIDS! I'M TAKING YOU TO NEW YORK CITY!
YAY!
YAY!
YAY!
YAY!*
YAY!
*Also yay backward

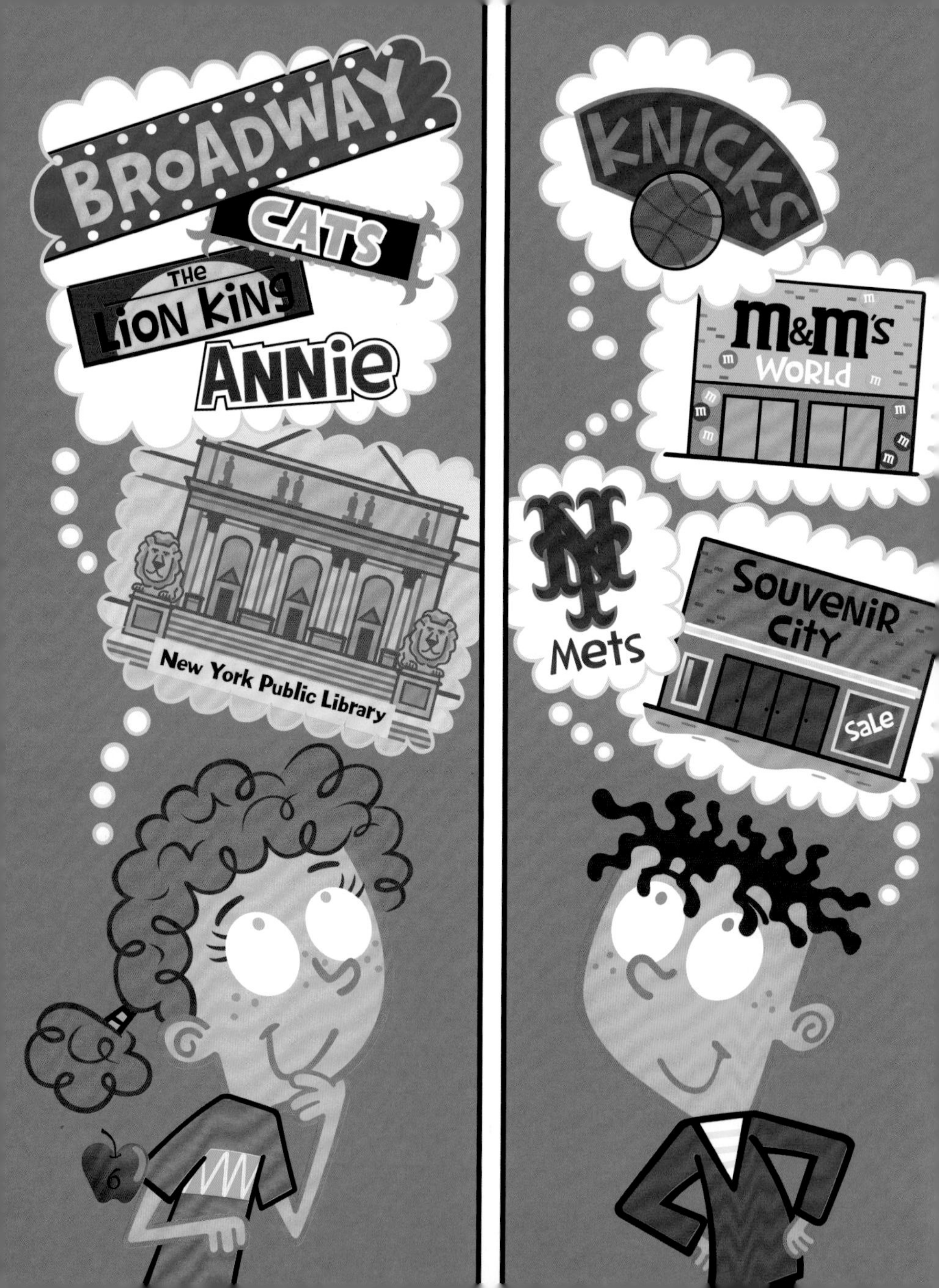
BROADWAY
CATS
THE LION KING
ANNIE
New York Public Library
KNICKS
M&M's
WORLD
Mets
SOUVENIR CITY
SALE

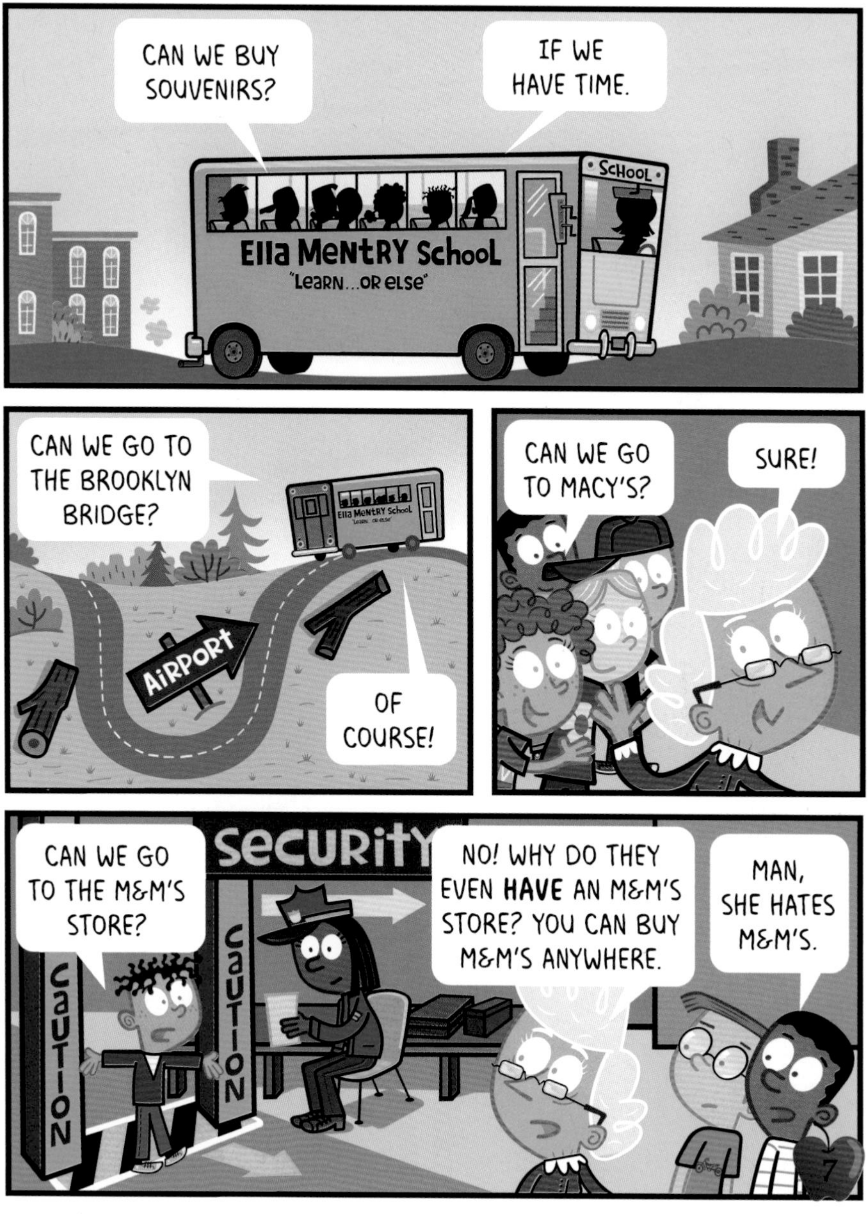

CAN WE BUY SOUVENIRS?
IF WE HAVE TIME.
SCHOOL
Ella MenTRY School
"LeaRN...OR eLSe"
CAN WE GO TO THE BROOKLYN BRIDGE?
AIRPORT
OF COURSE!
CAN WE GO TO MACY'S?
SURE!
CAN WE GO TO THE M&M'S STORE?
SECURITY
CAUTION
CAUTION
NO! WHY DO THEY EVEN **HAVE** AN M&M'S STORE? YOU CAN BUY M&M'S ANYWHERE.
MAN, SHE HATES M&M'S.

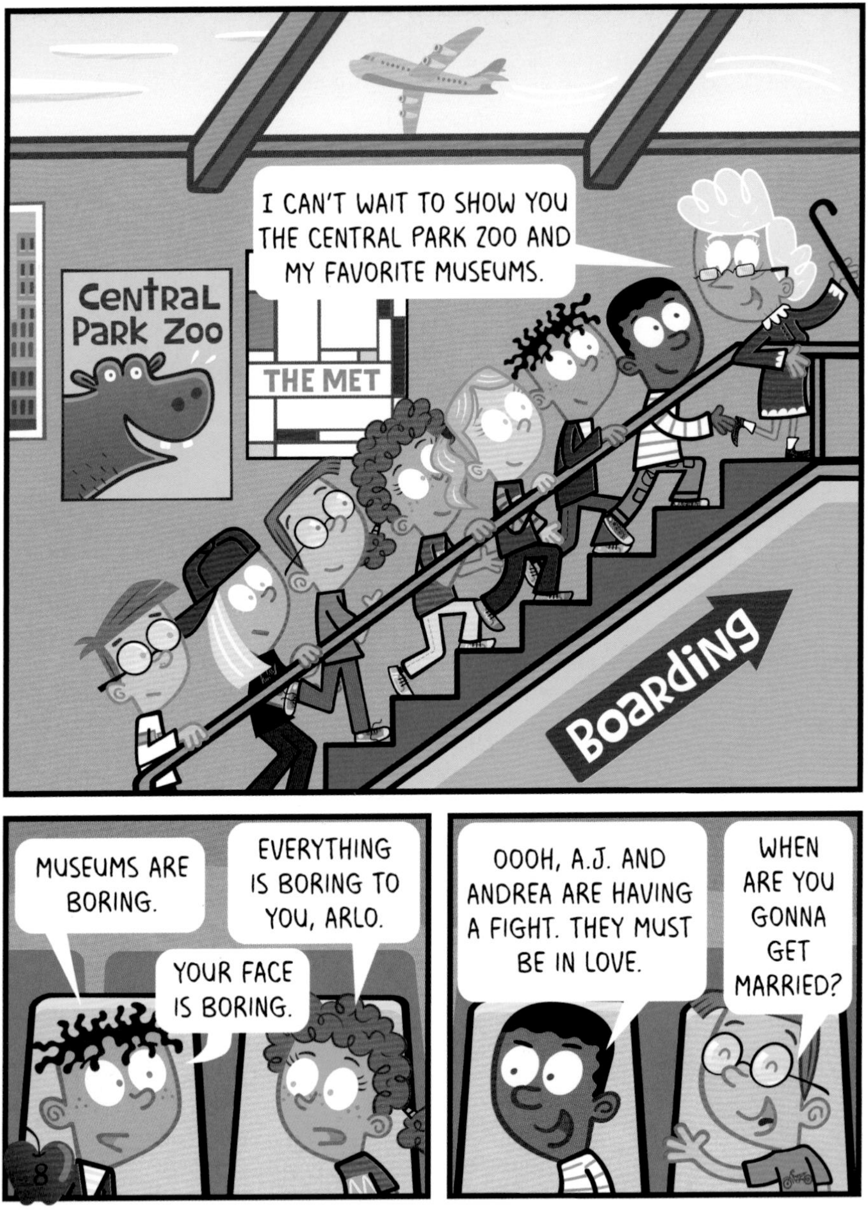
Central Park Zoo
THE MET
I CAN'T WAIT TO SHOW YOU THE CENTRAL PARK ZOO AND MY FAVORITE MUSEUMS.
Boarding
MUSEUMS ARE BORING.
EVERYTHING IS BORING TO YOU, ARLO.
YOUR FACE IS BORING.
OOOH, A.J. AND ANDREA ARE HAVING A FIGHT. THEY MUST BE IN LOVE.
WHEN ARE YOU GONNA GET MARRIED?

Weird Stuff about New York

IT'S A MISDEMEANOR TO FART IN NEW YORK CITY CHURCHES.

ALBERT EINSTEIN'S EYEBALLS ARE STORED IN A SAFE DEPOSIT BOX IN THE CITY.

THE EMPIRE STATE BUILDING HAS ITS OWN ZIP CODE.

MORE THAN 800 LANGUAGES ARE SPOKEN IN NEW YORK CITY.

NEW YORK CITY WAS THE FIRST CAPITAL OF THE UNITED STATES, IN 1789.

ONE OUT OF EVERY 38 PEOPLE IN THE UNITED STATES LIVES IN NEW YORK CITY.

THE FEDERAL RESERVE BANK HAS 7,000 TONS OF GOLD BARS, THE LARGEST GOLD STORAGE IN THE WORLD.

TIMES SQUARE WAS NAMED AFTER THE *NEW YORK TIMES*.

MORE PUERTO RICANS LIVE IN NEW YORK THAN IN ANY CITY IN PUERTO RICO.

INVENTED IN NEW YORK: ENGLISH MUFFINS, JELL-O, POTATO CHIPS, TOILET PAPER, AIR-CONDITIONING, THE TUXEDO, EGGS BENEDICT, CHEWING GUM, TEDDY BEARS, SCRABBLE, HOT DOGS, HIP-HOP, MR. POTATO HEAD

275 SPECIES OF BIRDS HAVE BEEN SPOTTED IN CENTRAL PARK.

THAT'S WEIRD.

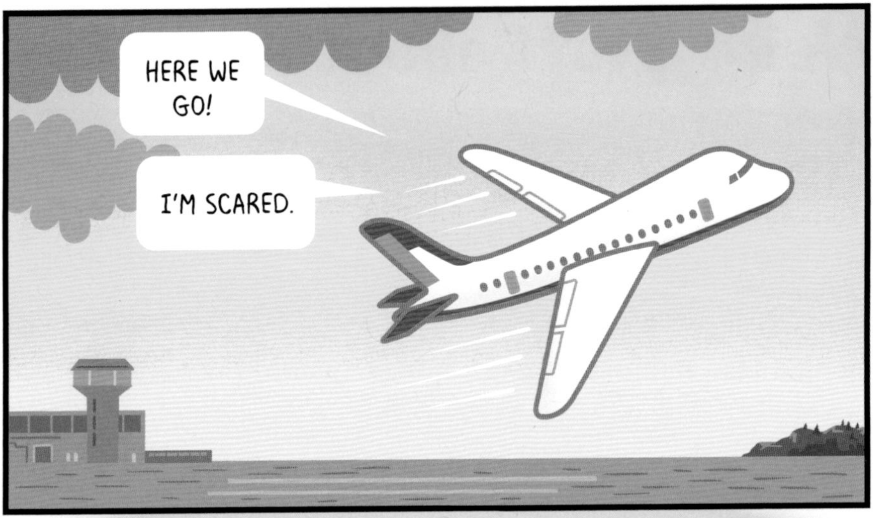
HERE WE GO!
I'M SCARED.

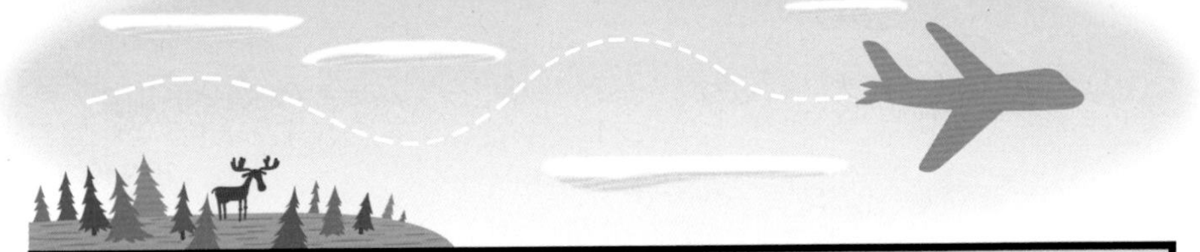

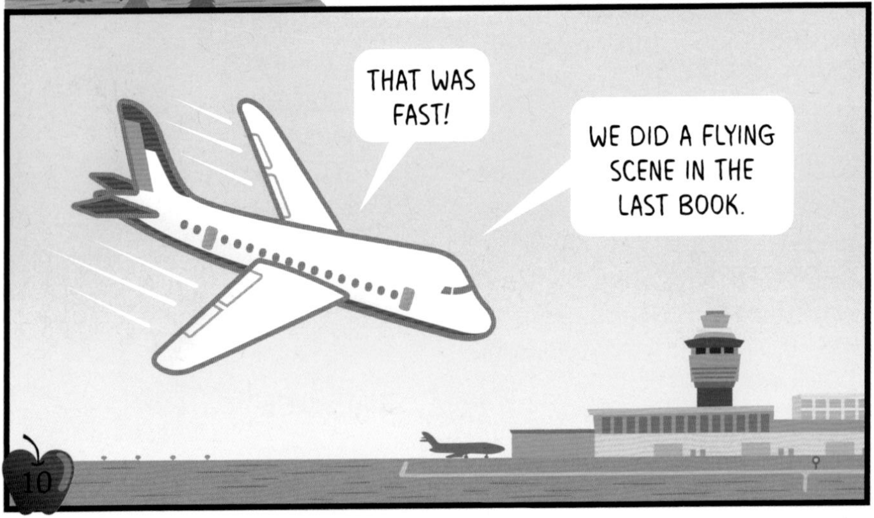
THAT WAS FAST!
WE DID A FLYING SCENE IN THE LAST BOOK.

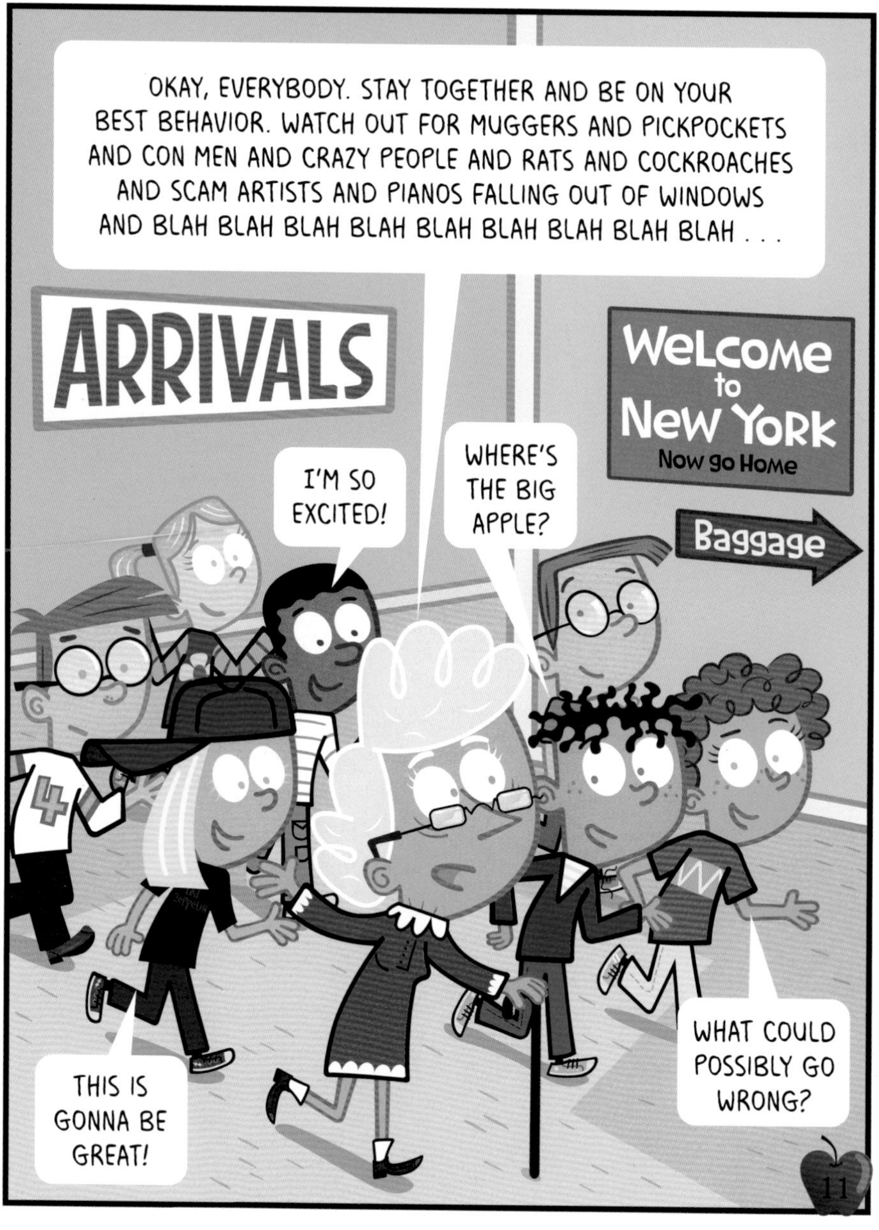
OKAY, EVERYBODY. STAY TOGETHER AND BE ON YOUR BEST BEHAVIOR. WATCH OUT FOR MUGGERS AND PICKPOCKETS AND CON MEN AND CRAZY PEOPLE AND RATS AND COCKROACHES AND SCAM ARTISTS AND PIANOS FALLING OUT OF WINDOWS AND BLAH BLAH BLAH BLAH BLAH BLAH BLAH BLAH BLAH . . .
ARRIVALS
Welcome to New York
Now go Home
I'M SO EXCITED!
WHERE'S THE BIG APPLE?
Baggage
THIS IS GONNA BE GREAT!
WHAT COULD POSSIBLY GO WRONG?

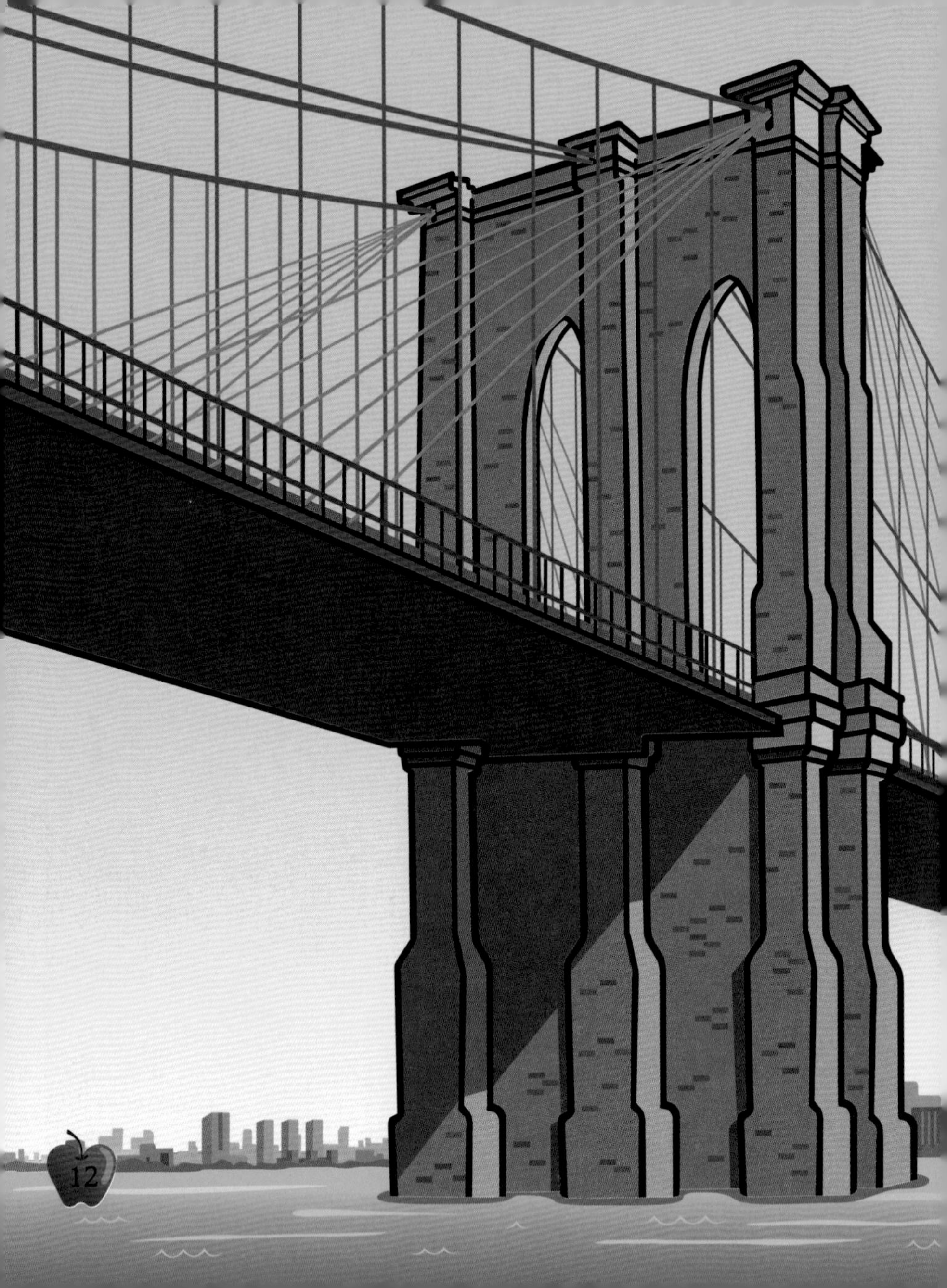

CHAPTER 2

People Who Don't Flush the Toilet

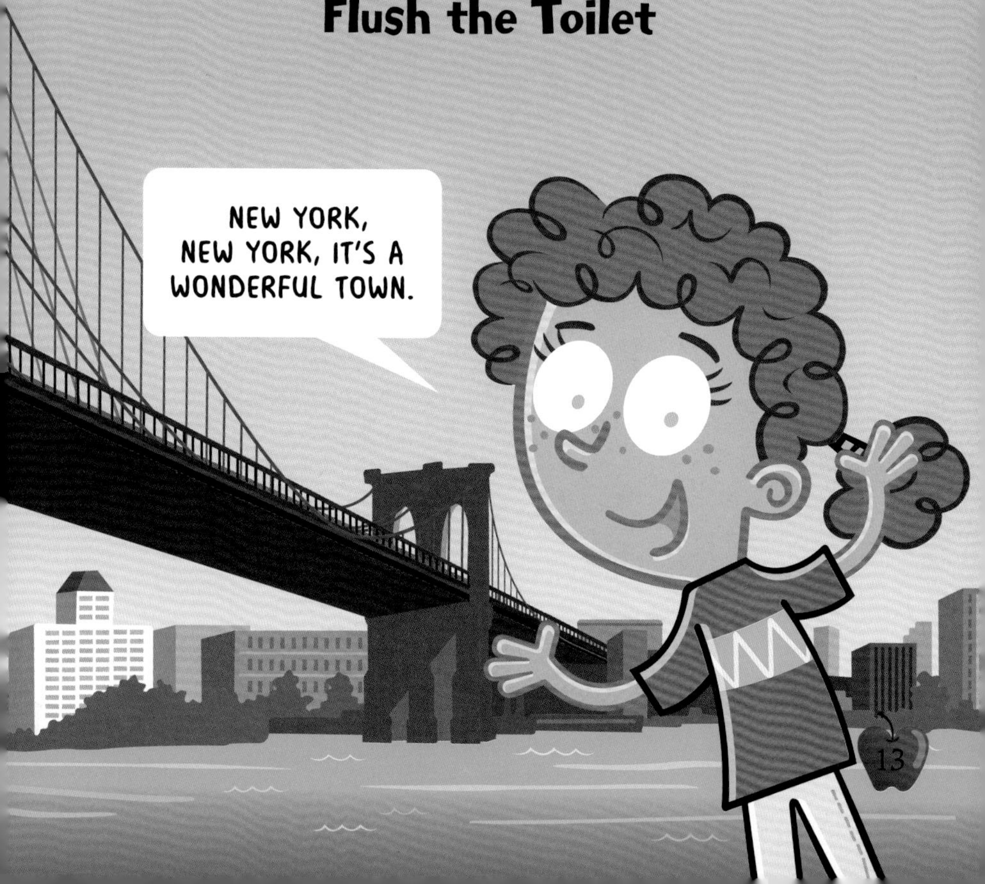

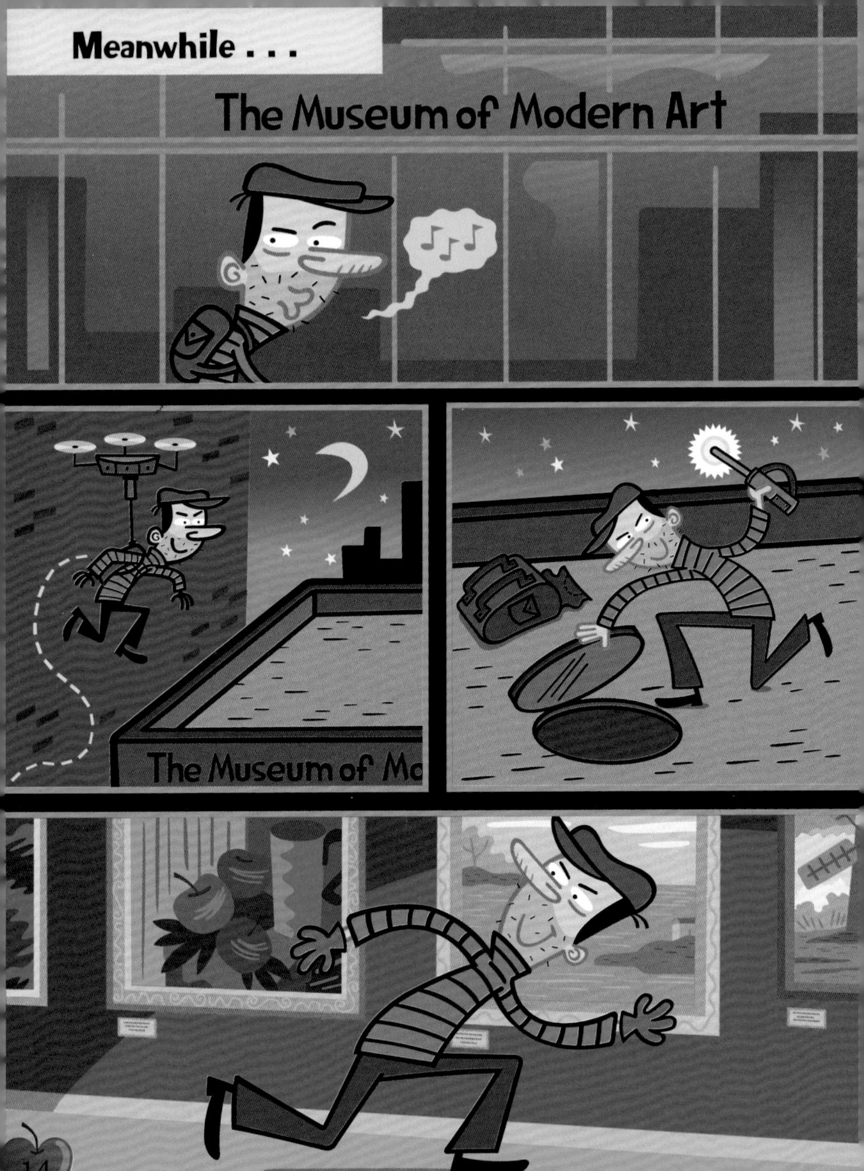
Meanwhile . . .
The Museum of Modern Art
The Museum of Mo

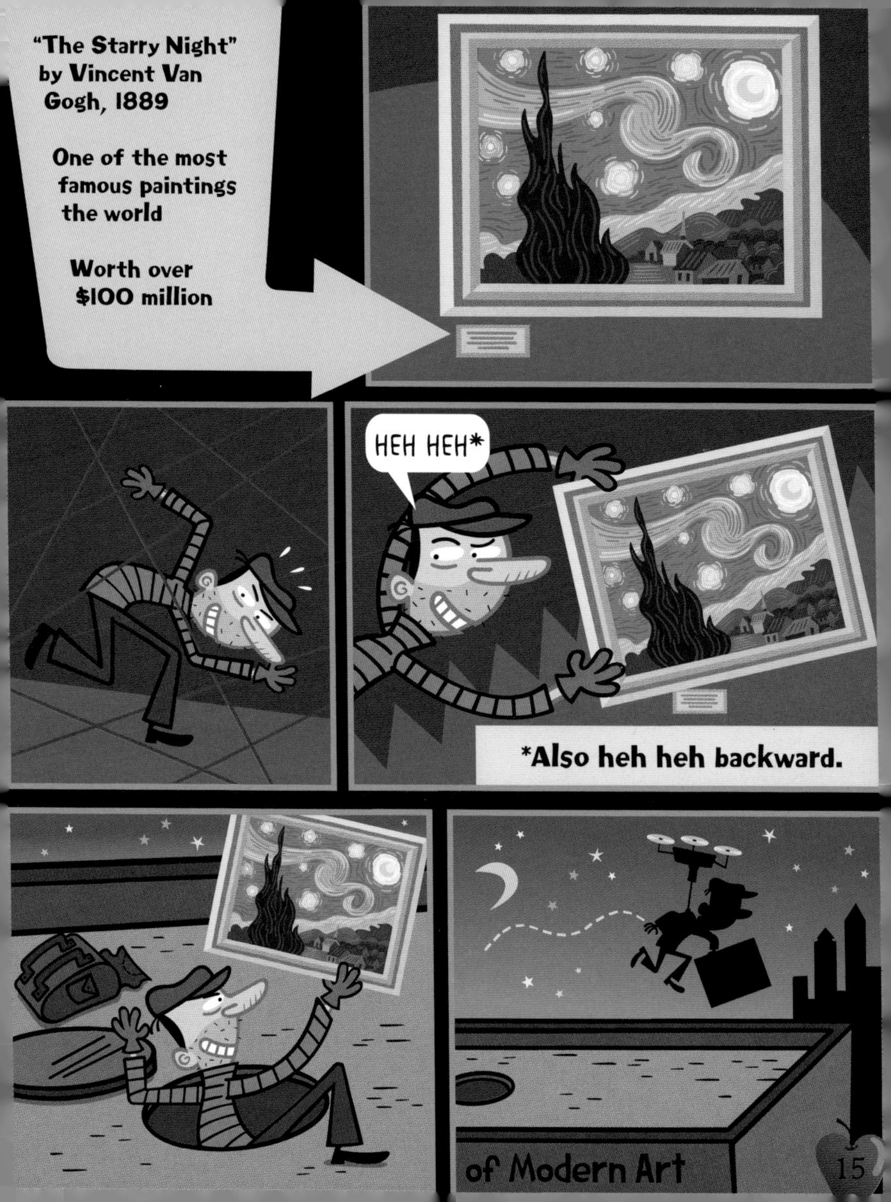

"The Starry Night" by Vincent Van Gogh, 1889
One of the most famous paintings the world
Worth over $100 million
HEH HEH*
*Also heh heh backward.
of Modern Art

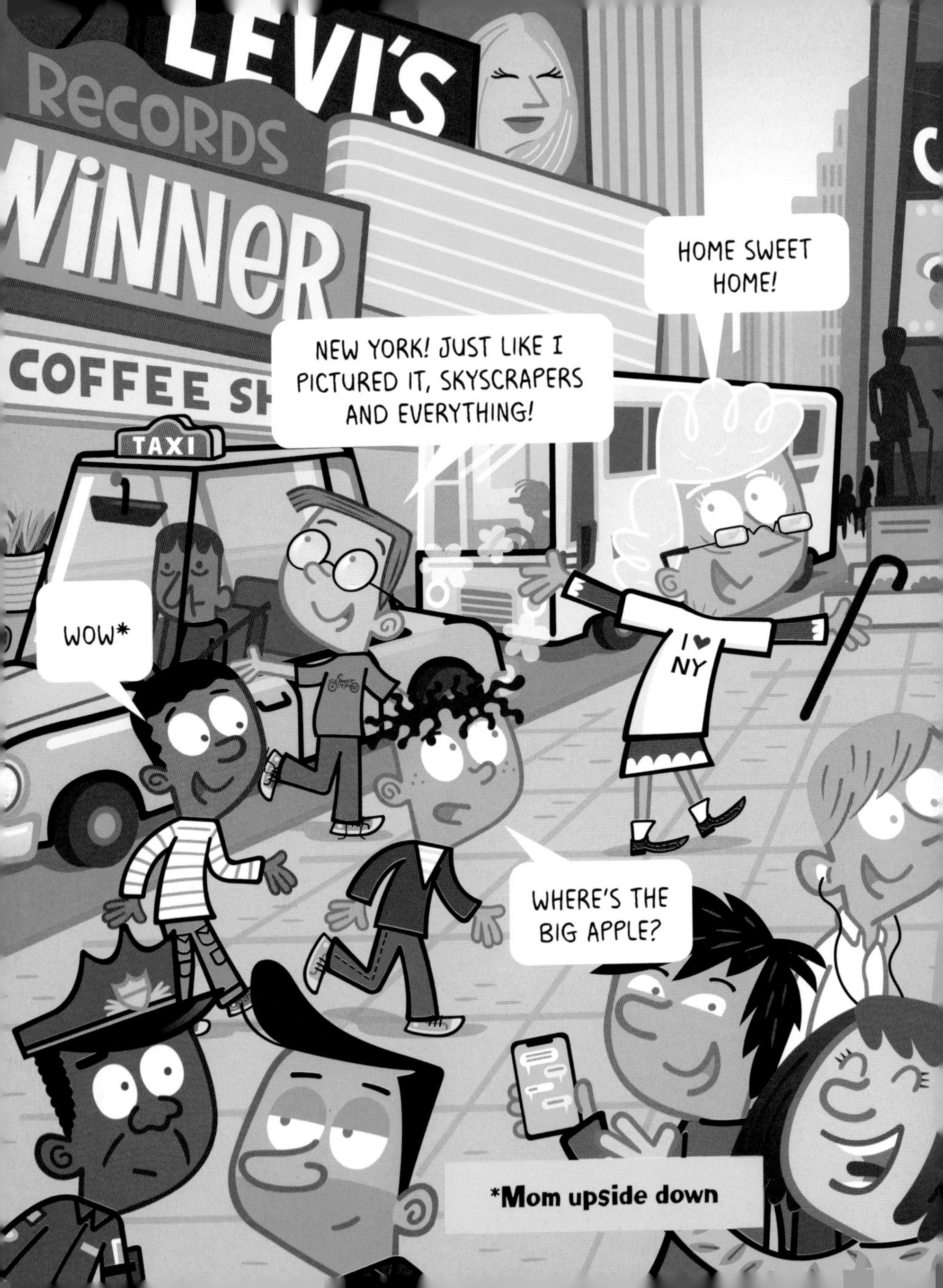
LEVI'S
RECORDS
WINNER
COFFEE SH
TAXI
HOME SWEET HOME!
NEW YORK! JUST LIKE I PICTURED IT, SKYSCRAPERS AND EVERYTHING!
WOW*
I ♥ NY
WHERE'S THE BIG APPLE?
*Mom upside down

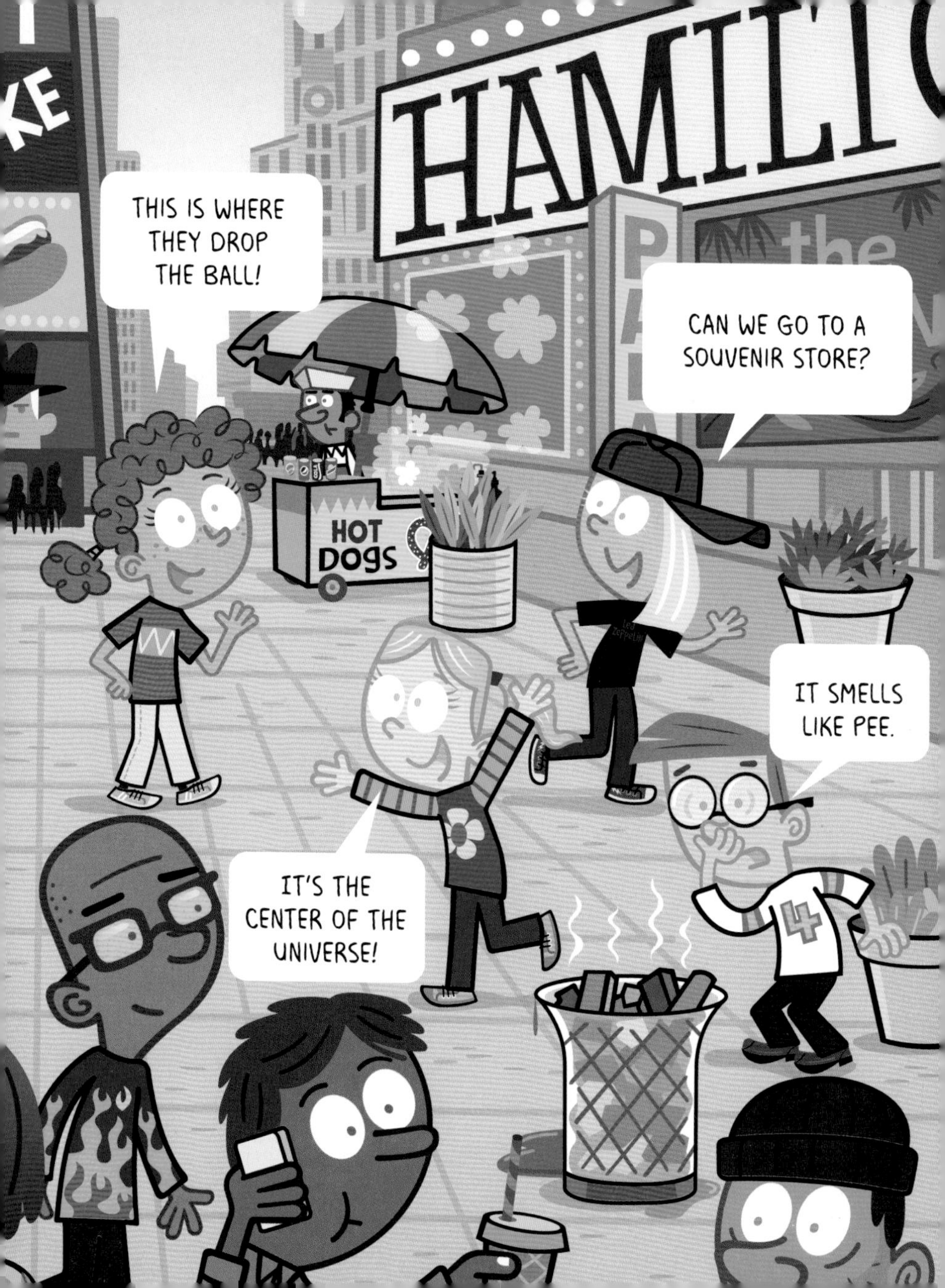
THIS IS WHERE THEY DROP THE BALL!
CAN WE GO TO A SOUVENIR STORE?
IT SMELLS LIKE PEE.
IT'S THE CENTER OF THE UNIVERSE!
HOT DOGS

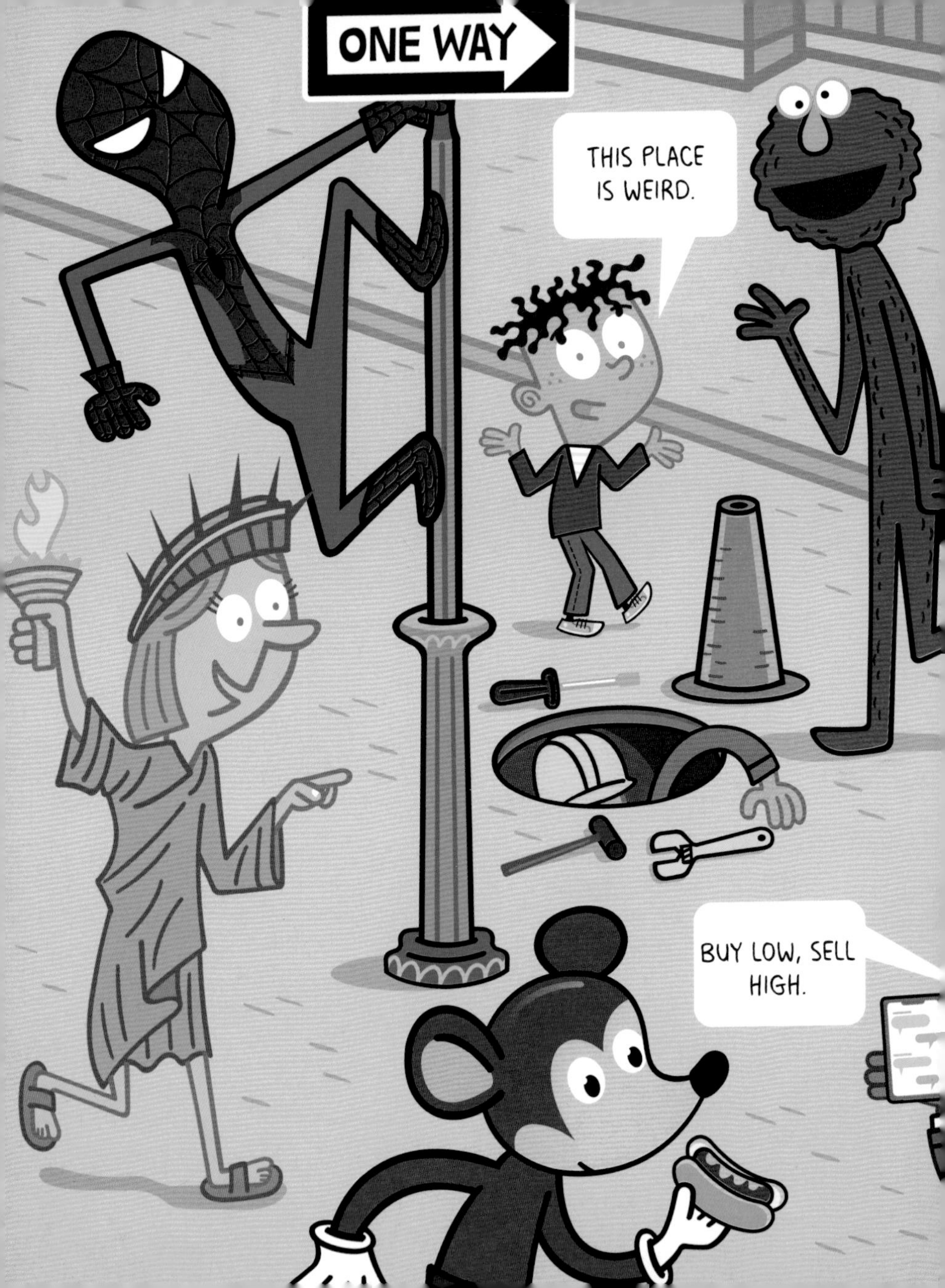
ONE WAY
THIS PLACE IS WEIRD.
BUY LOW, SELL HIGH.

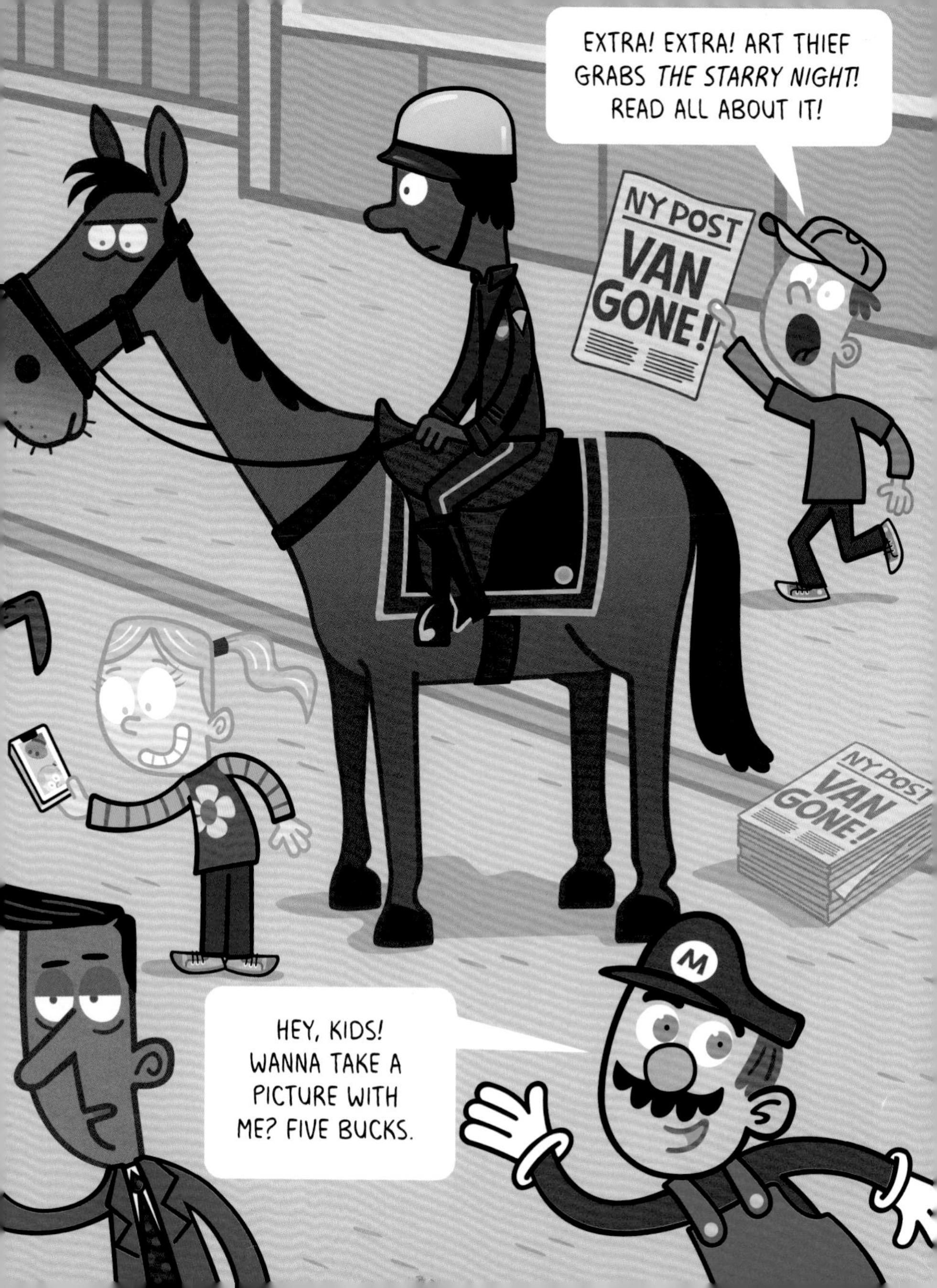
EXTRA! EXTRA! ART THIEF GRABS THE STARRY NIGHT! READ ALL ABOUT IT!
NY POST
VAN GONE!
NY POST
VAN GONE!
M
HEY, KIDS! WANNA TAKE A PICTURE WITH ME? FIVE BUCKS.

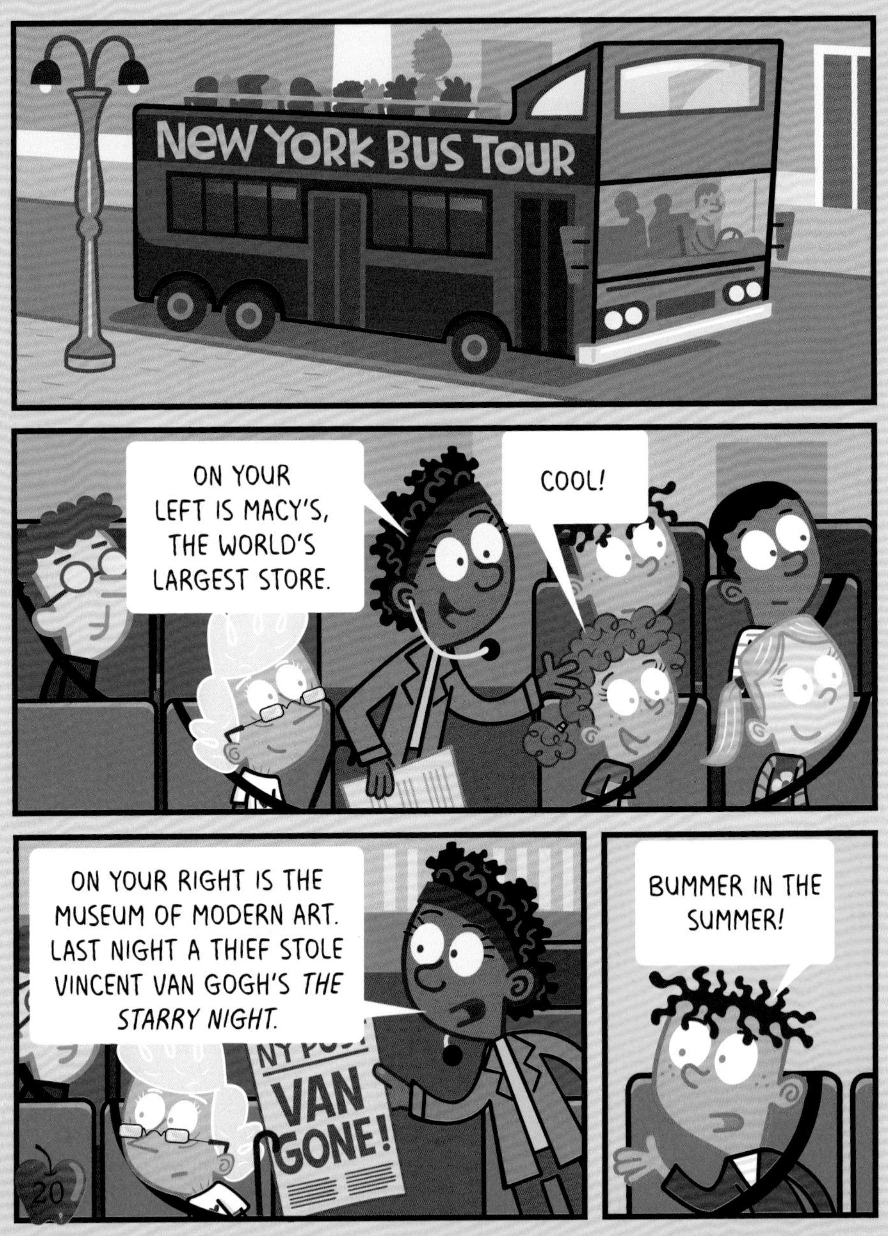
NEW YORK BUS TOUR
ON YOUR LEFT IS MACY'S, THE WORLD'S LARGEST STORE.
COOL!
ON YOUR RIGHT IS THE MUSEUM OF MODERN ART. LAST NIGHT A THIEF STOLE VINCENT VAN GOGH'S *THE STARRY NIGHT.*
NY POST
VAN GONE!
BUMMER IN THE SUMMER!

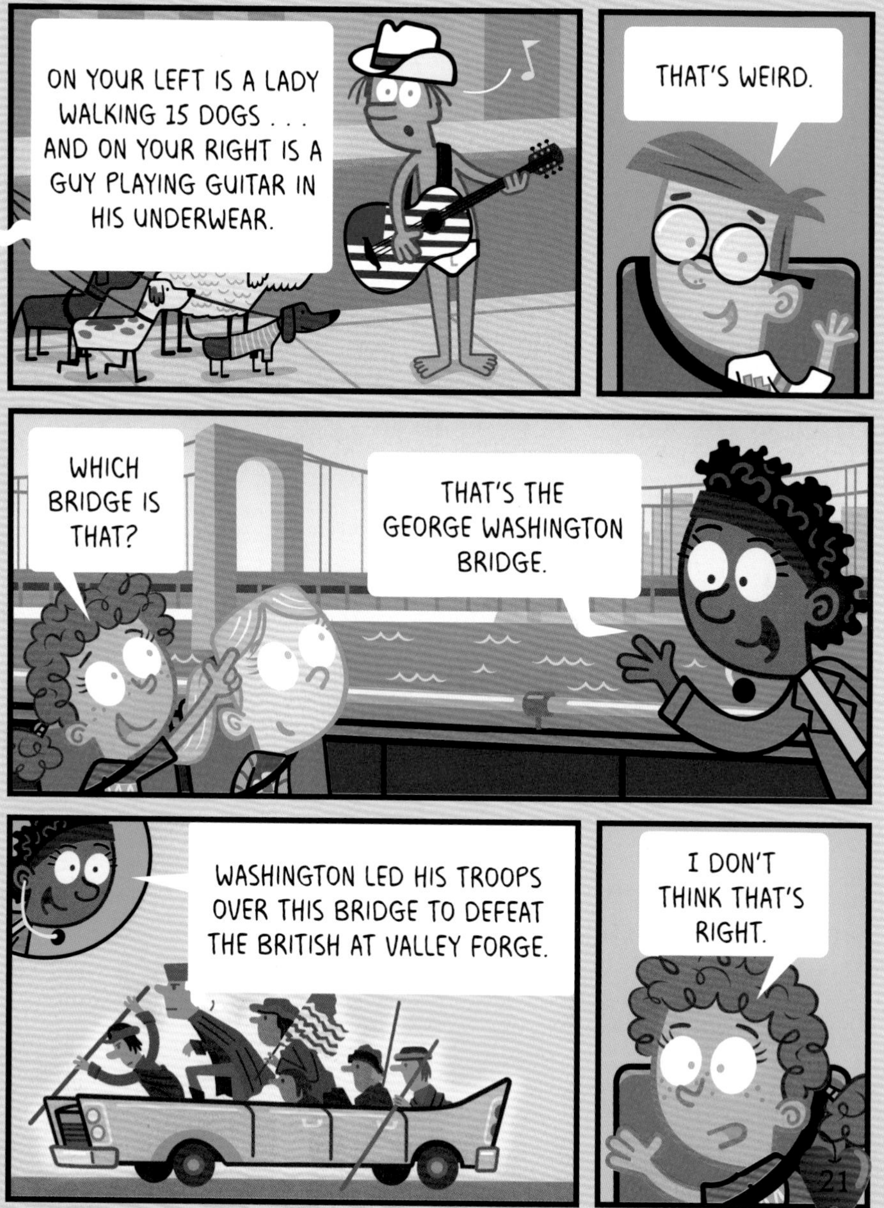
ON YOUR LEFT IS A LADY WALKING 15 DOGS . . . AND ON YOUR RIGHT IS A GUY PLAYING GUITAR IN HIS UNDERWEAR.
THAT'S WEIRD.
WHICH BRIDGE IS THAT?
THAT'S THE GEORGE WASHINGTON BRIDGE.
WASHINGTON LED HIS TROOPS OVER THIS BRIDGE TO DEFEAT THE BRITISH AT VALLEY FORGE.
I DON'T THINK THAT'S RIGHT.

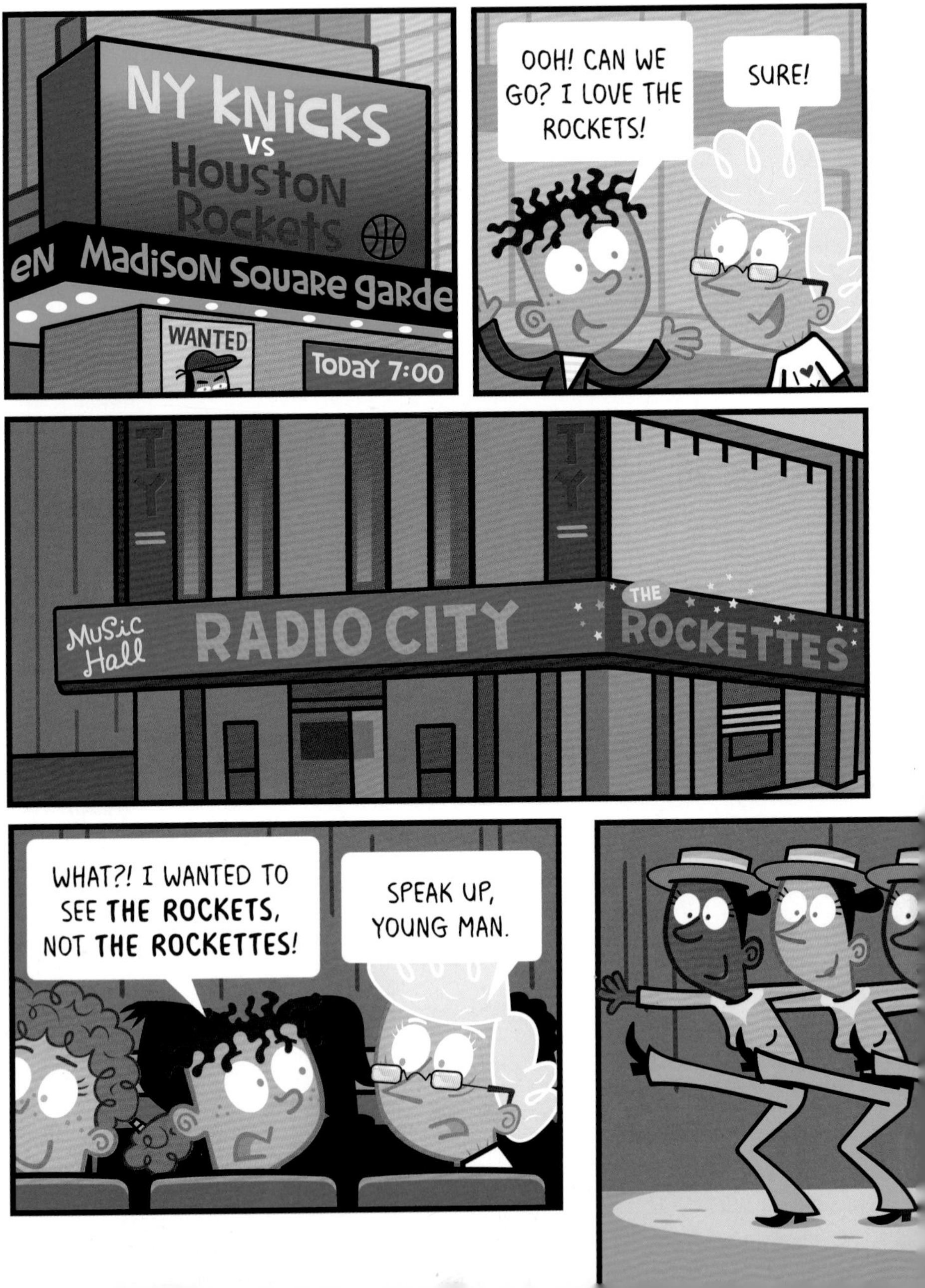
NY KNICKS
VS
HOUSTON
ROCKETS
EN MADISON SQUARE GARDE
WANTED
TODAY 7:00
OOH! CAN WE GO? I LOVE THE ROCKETS!
SURE!
MUSIC HALL
RADIO CITY
THE ROCKETTES
WHAT?! I WANTED TO SEE **THE ROCKETS**, NOT **THE ROCKETTES**!
SPEAK UP, YOUNG MAN.

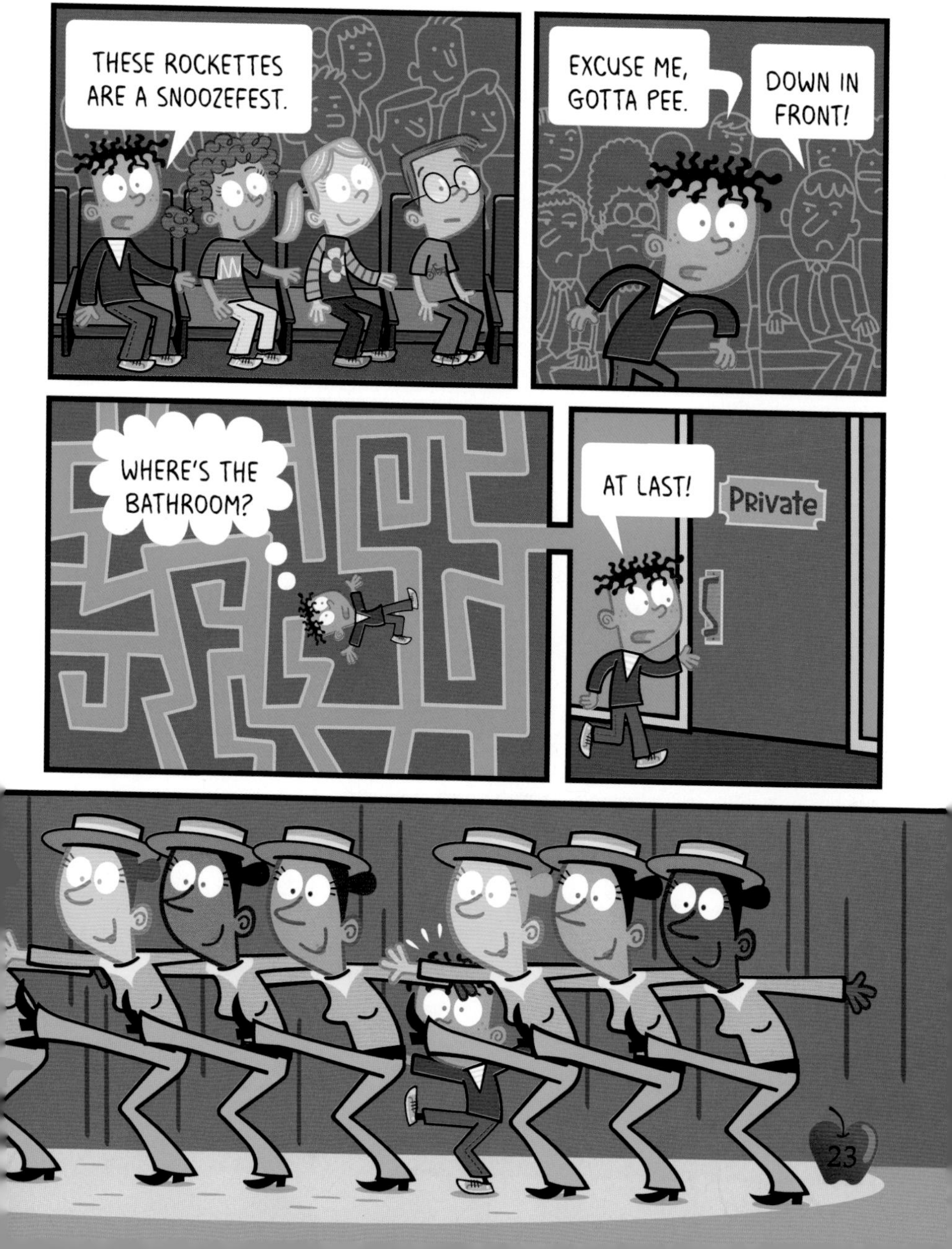
THESE ROCKETTES ARE A SNOOZEFEST.
EXCUSE ME, GOTTA PEE.
DOWN IN FRONT!
WHERE'S THE BATHROOM?
AT LAST!
Private

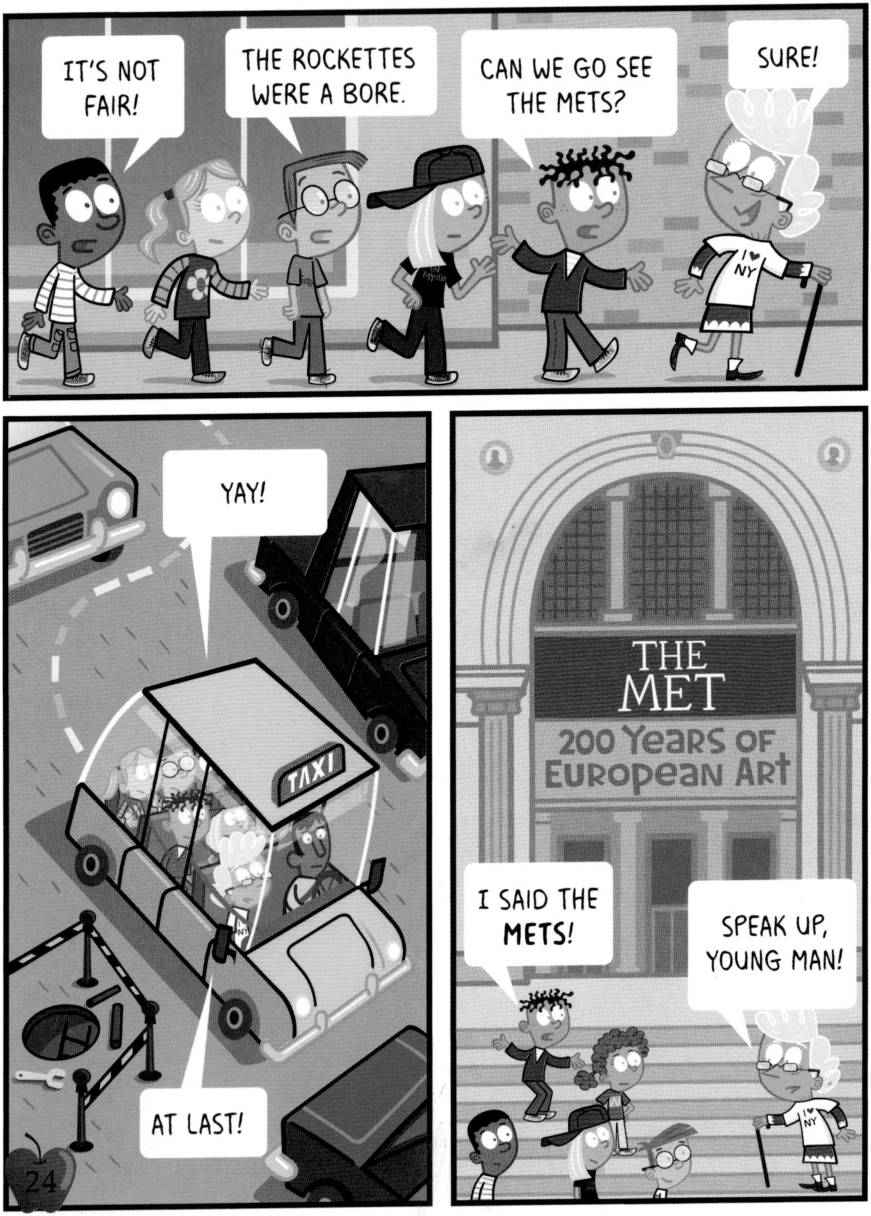
IT'S NOT FAIR!
THE ROCKETTES WERE A BORE.
CAN WE GO SEE THE METS?
SURE!
YAY!
TAXI
AT LAST!
THE MET
200 Years of European Art
I SAID THE **METS**!
SPEAK UP, YOUNG MAN!

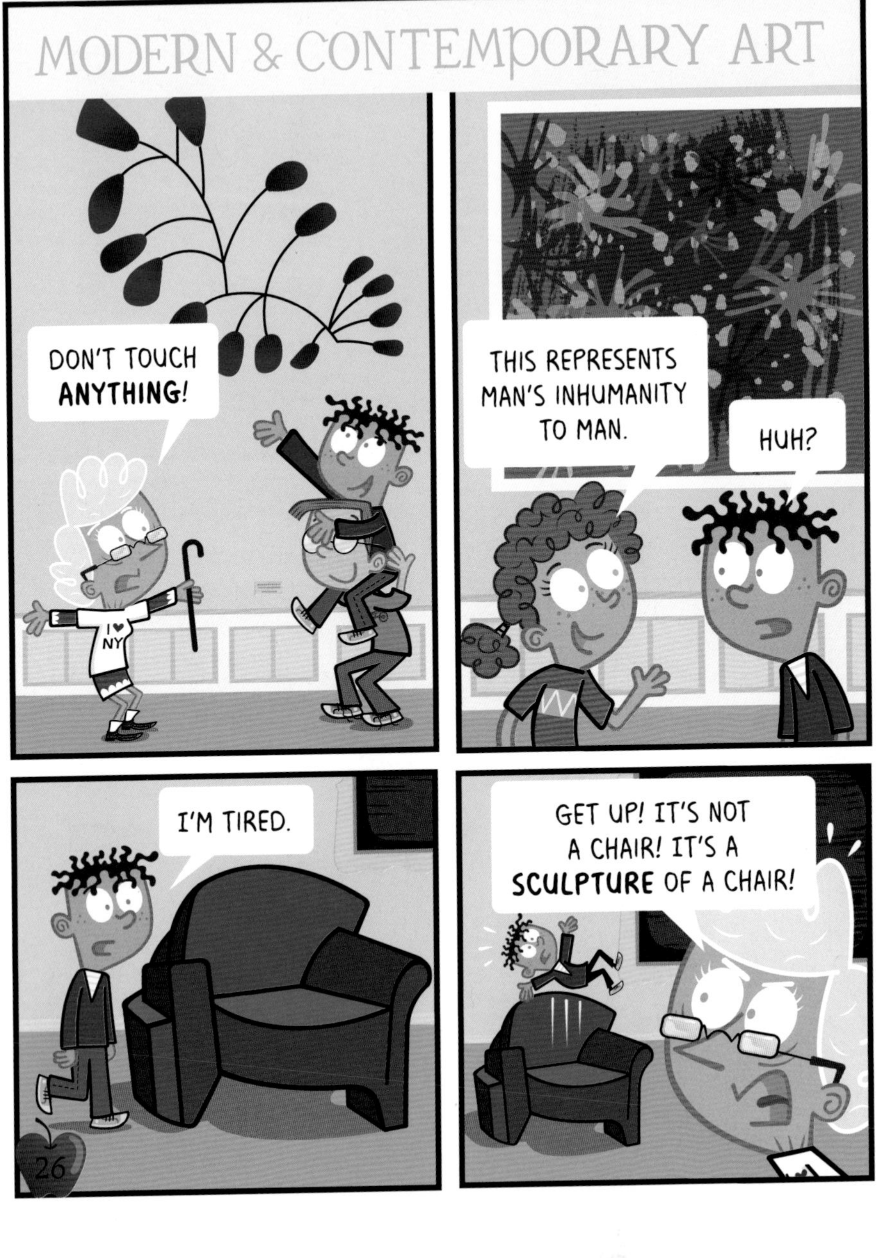
MODERN & CONTEMPORARY ART
DON'T TOUCH **ANYTHING!**
I ♥ NY
THIS REPRESENTS MAN'S INHUMANITY TO MAN.
HUH?
I'M TIRED.
GET UP! IT'S NOT A CHAIR! IT'S A **SCULPTURE** OF A CHAIR!

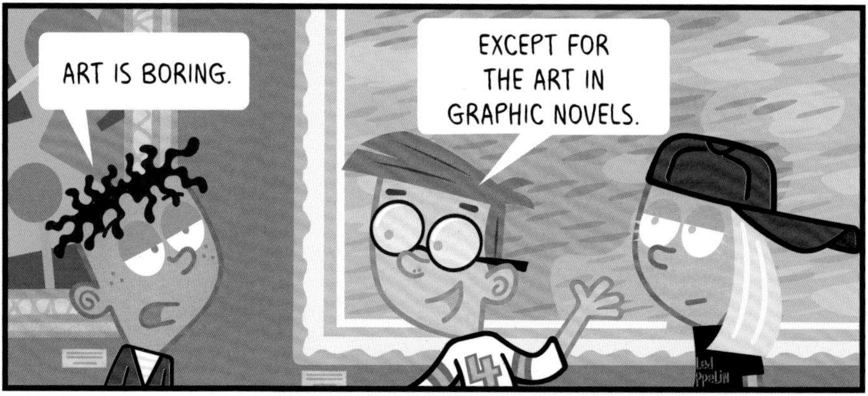
ART IS BORING.
EXCEPT FOR THE ART IN GRAPHIC NOVELS.

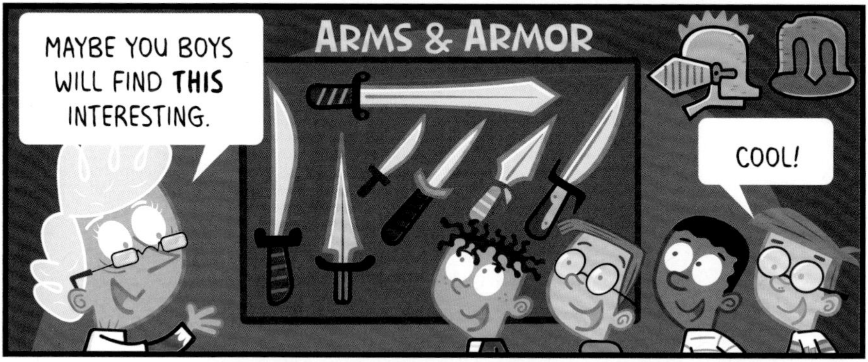
ARMS & ARMOR
MAYBE YOU BOYS WILL FIND **THIS** INTERESTING.
COOL!

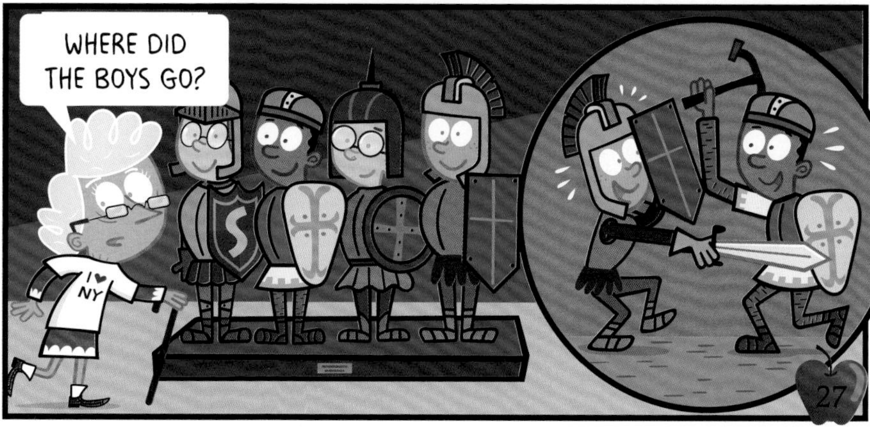
WHERE DID THE BOYS GO?
I ♥ NY

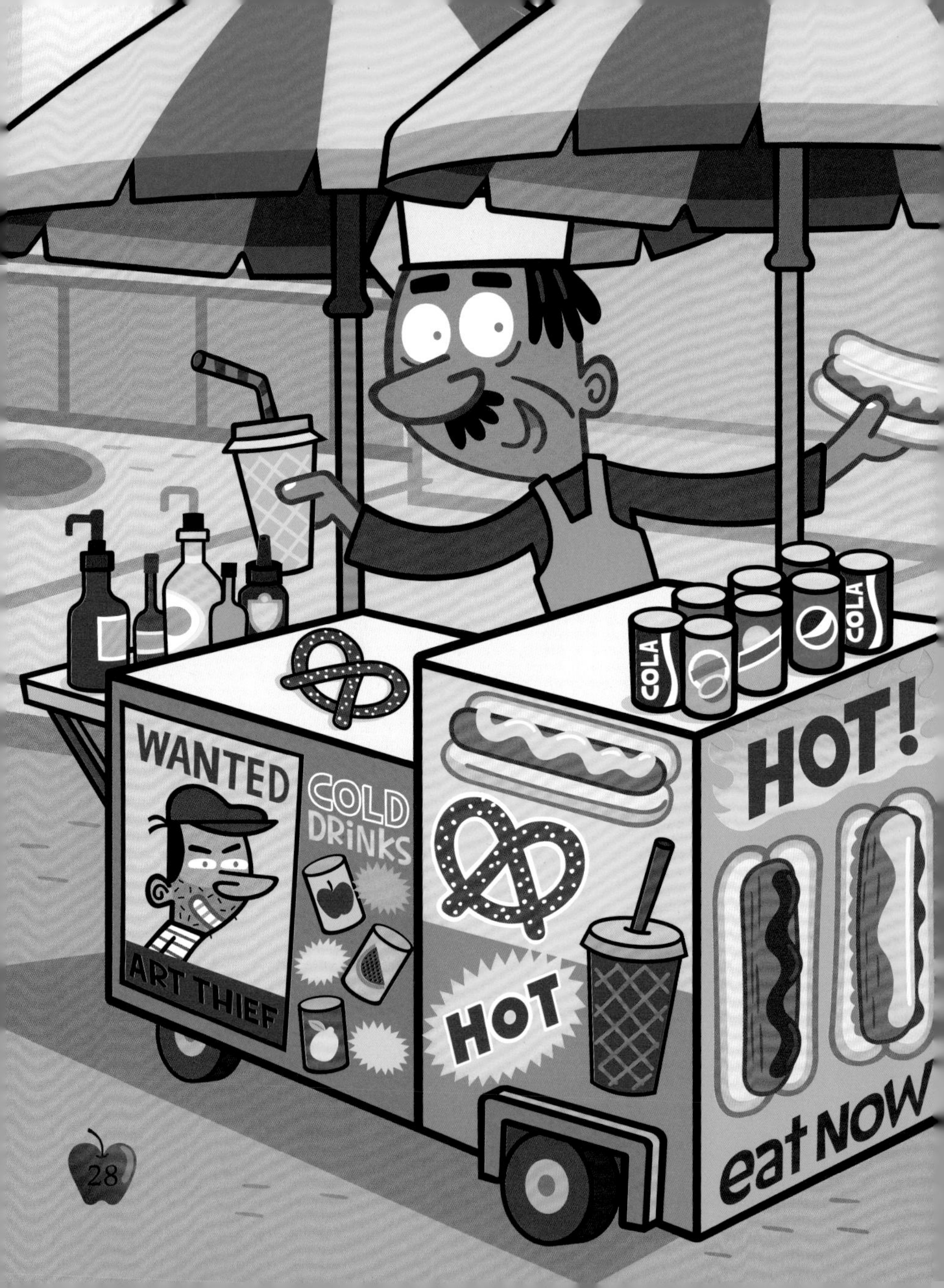
COLA
COLA
WANTED
ART THIEF
COLD DRINKS
HOT!
HOT
eat NOW

CHAPTER 3

People Who Stop at the Bottom of an Escalator and Just Stand There

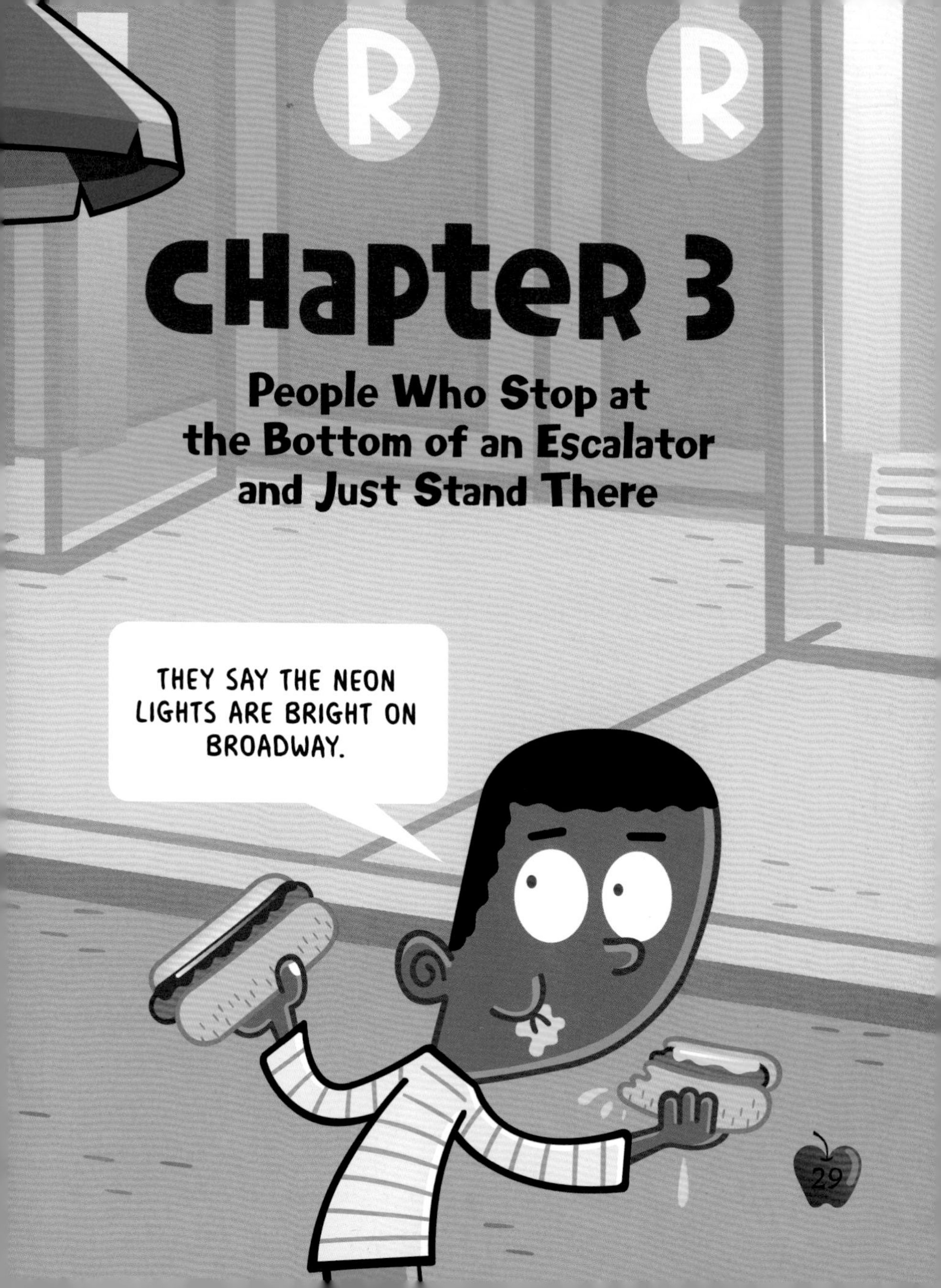

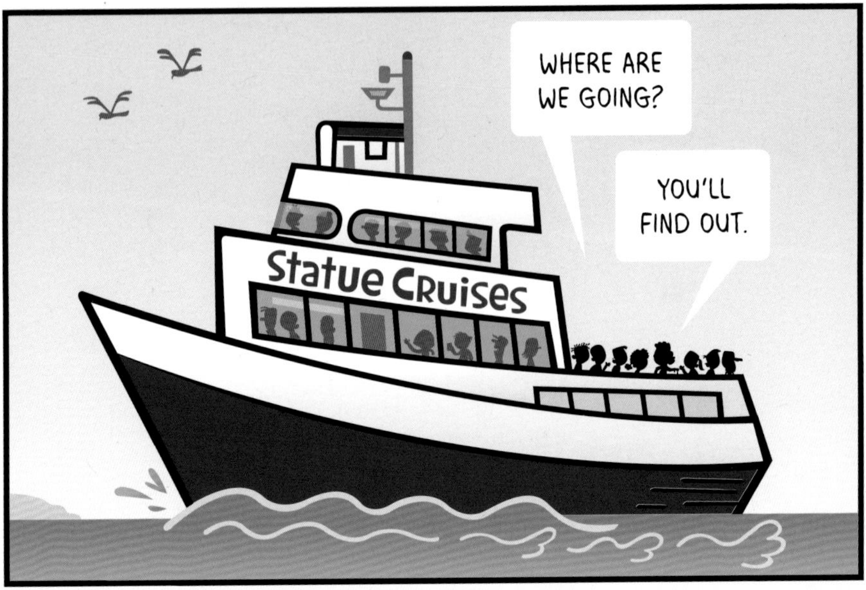
WHERE ARE WE GOING?
YOU'LL FIND OUT.
Statue Cruises

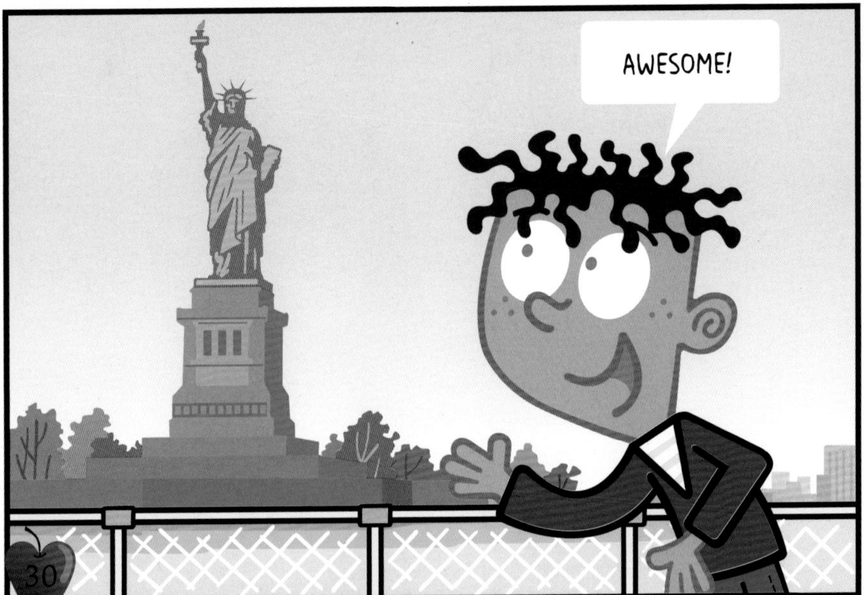
AWESOME!

Weird Stuff about the Statue of Liberty

SHE GETS STRUCK BY LIGHTNING 600 TIMES A YEAR.

HER FACE IS MODELED AFTER THE SCULPTOR'S MOTHER.

HER SPIKY CROWN REPRESENTS THE SEVEN OCEANS AND SEVEN CONTINENTS.

THE SHIP CARRYING HER ALMOST SANK ON ITS WAY TO AMERICA.

SHE'S GREEN BECAUSE OF THE OXIDATION OF COPPER.

IN 1886, SHE WAS THE TALLEST IRON STRUCTURE IN THE WORLD.

IN HIGH WINDS, SHE CAN SWAY THREE INCHES.

HER WAISTLINE IS 35 FEET.

SHE'S ACTUALLY CLOSER TO NEW JERSEY THAN NEW YORK.

HER SHOE SIZE IS 879.

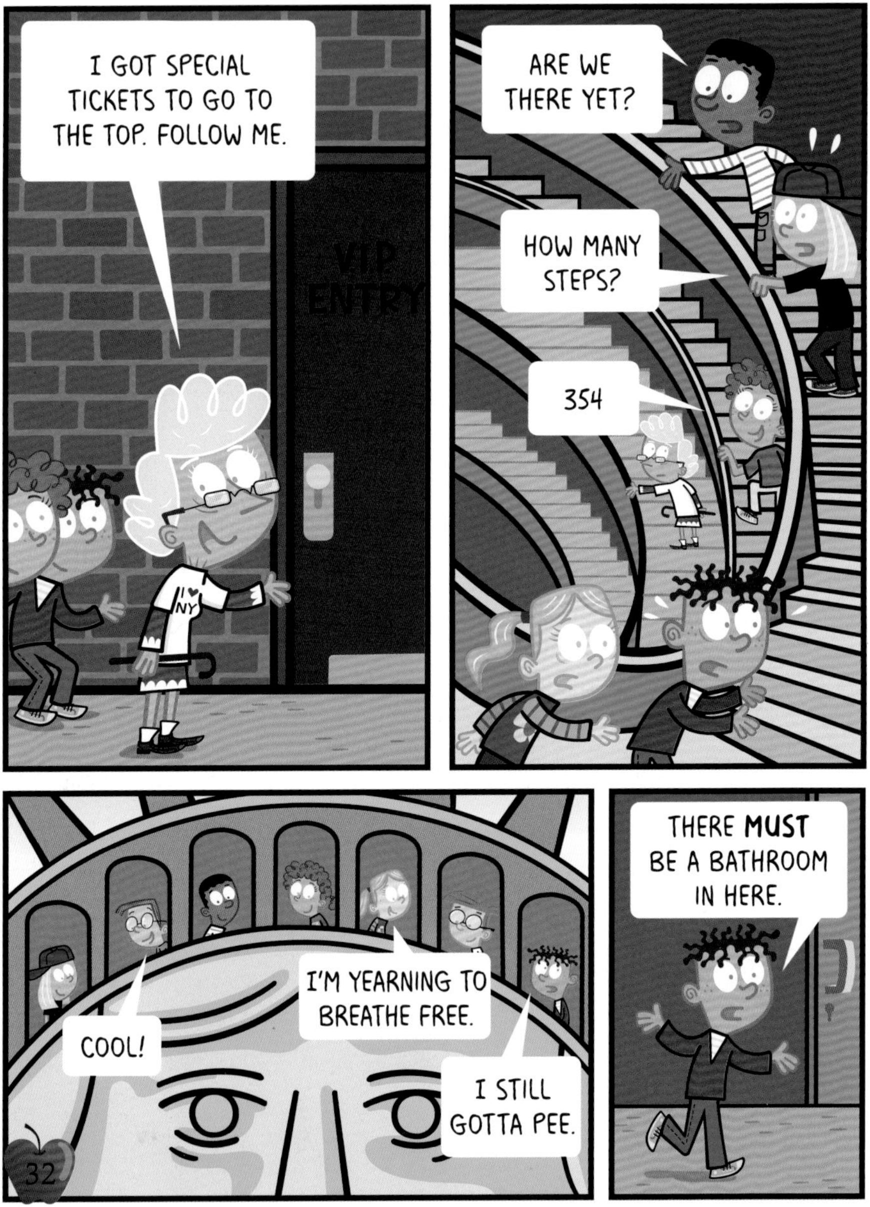

I GOT SPECIAL TICKETS TO GO TO THE TOP. FOLLOW ME.
VIP ENTRY
ARE WE THERE YET?
HOW MANY STEPS?
354
COOL!
I'M YEARNING TO BREATHE FREE.
I STILL GOTTA PEE.
THERE **MUST** BE A BATHROOM IN HERE.

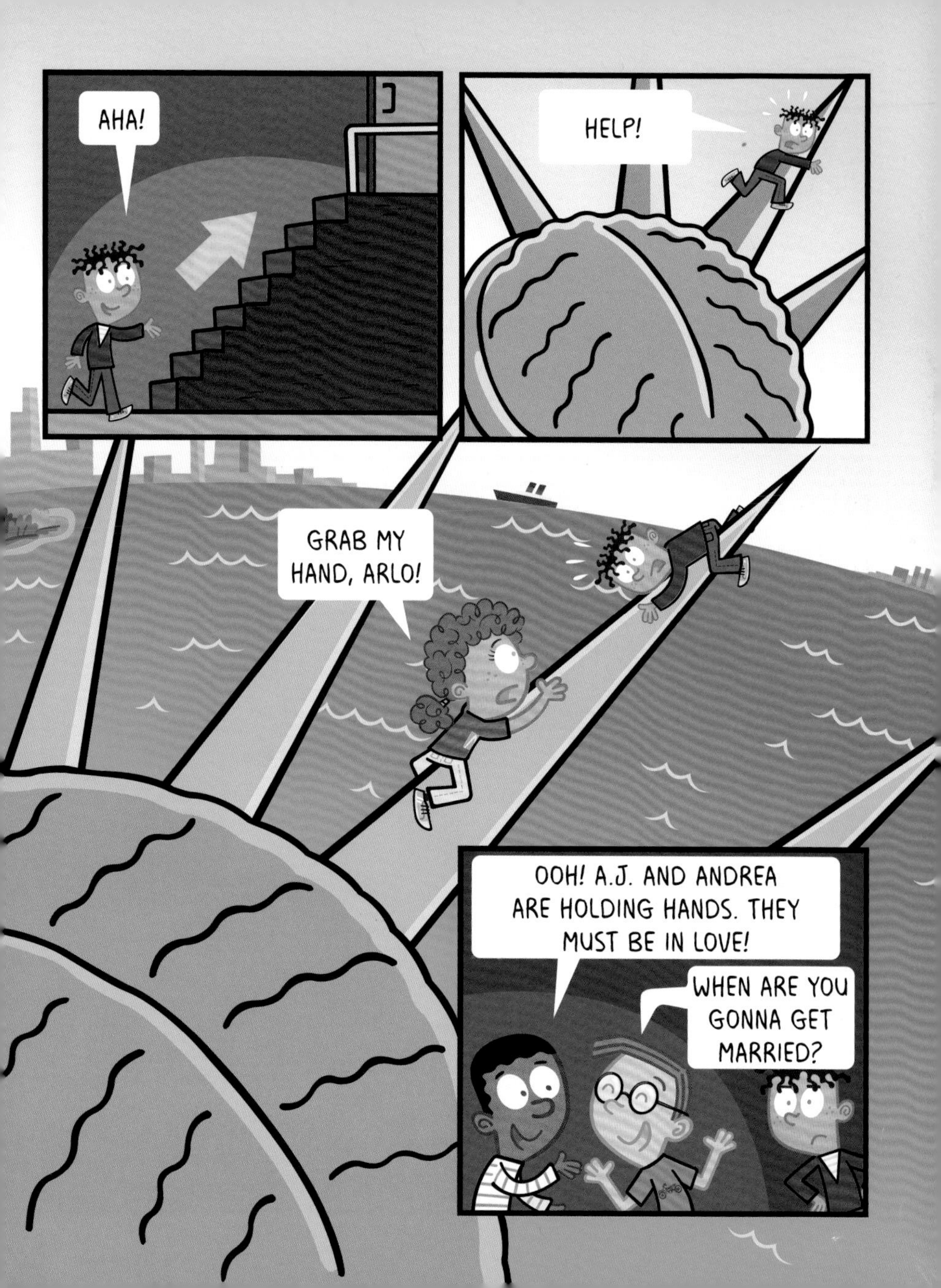

AHA!
HELP!
GRAB MY HAND, ARLO!
OOH! A.J. AND ANDREA ARE HOLDING HANDS. THEY MUST BE IN LOVE!
WHEN ARE YOU GONNA GET MARRIED?

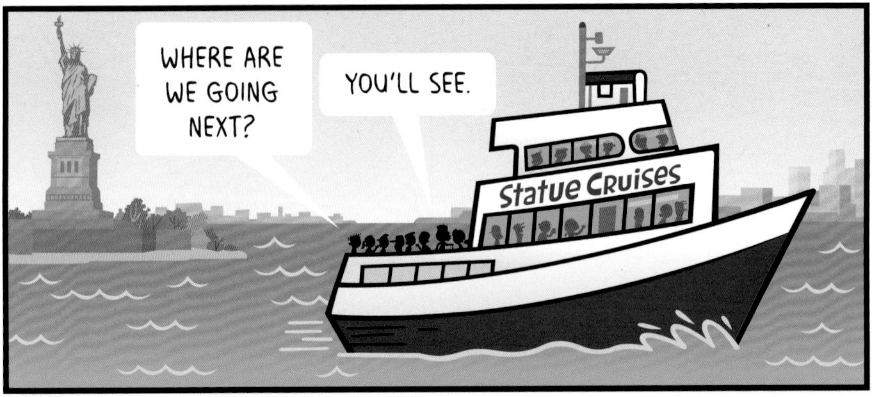
WHERE ARE WE GOING NEXT?
YOU'LL SEE.
Statue Cruises

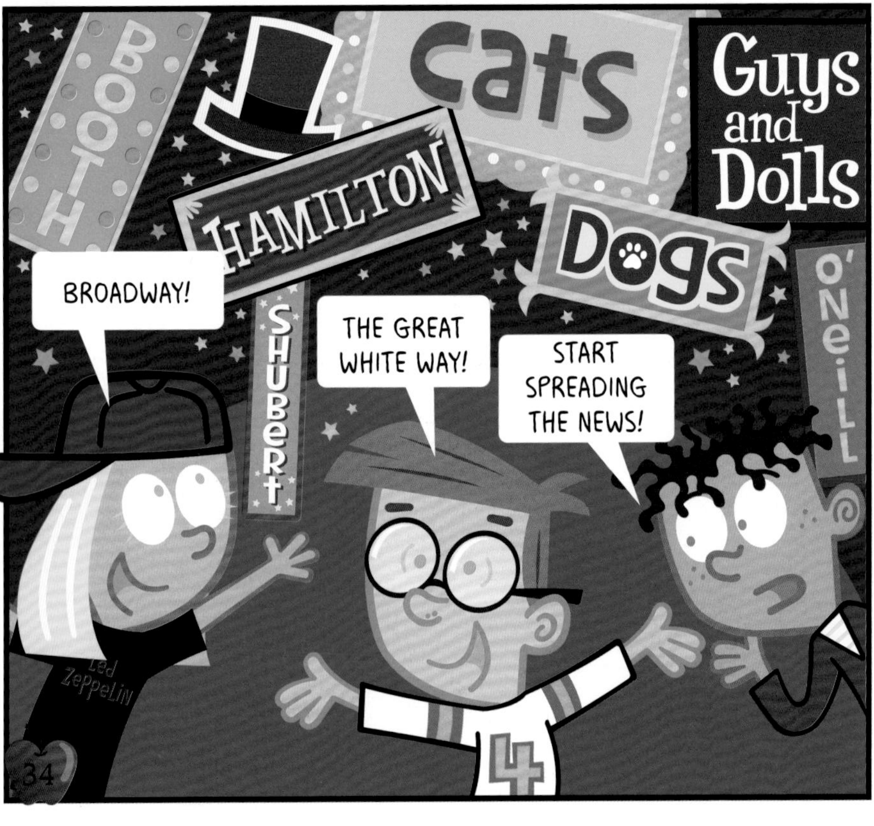
BOOTH
Cats
Guys and Dolls
HAMILTON
Dogs
O'NeiLL
SHUBERT
BROADWAY!
THE GREAT WHITE WAY!
START SPREADING THE NEWS!
Led ZePPeLIN
4

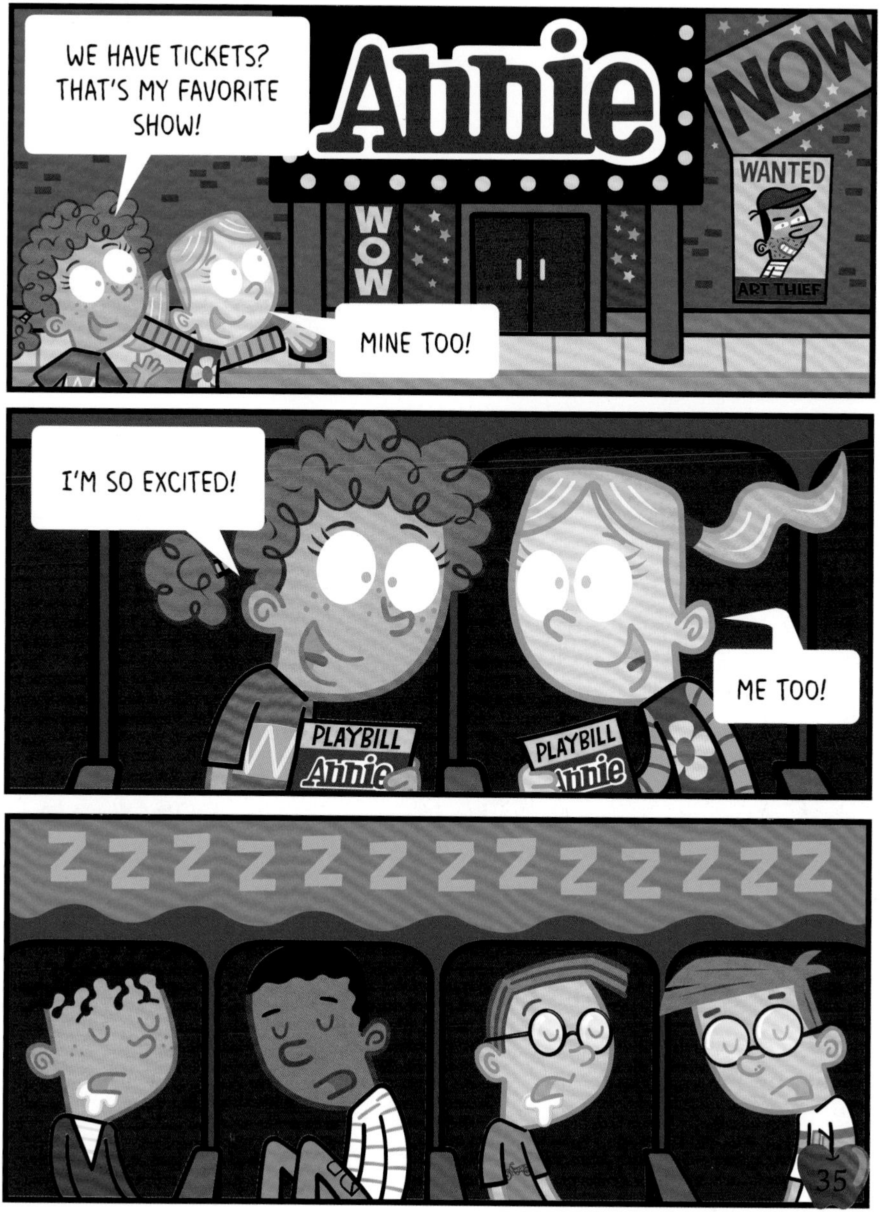
WE HAVE TICKETS? THAT'S MY FAVORITE SHOW!
Annie
NOW
WOW
WANTED
ART THIEF
MINE TOO!
I'M SO EXCITED!
ME TOO!
PLAYBILL
Annie
PLAYBILL
Annie
Z Z Z Z Z Z Z Z Z Z Z Z

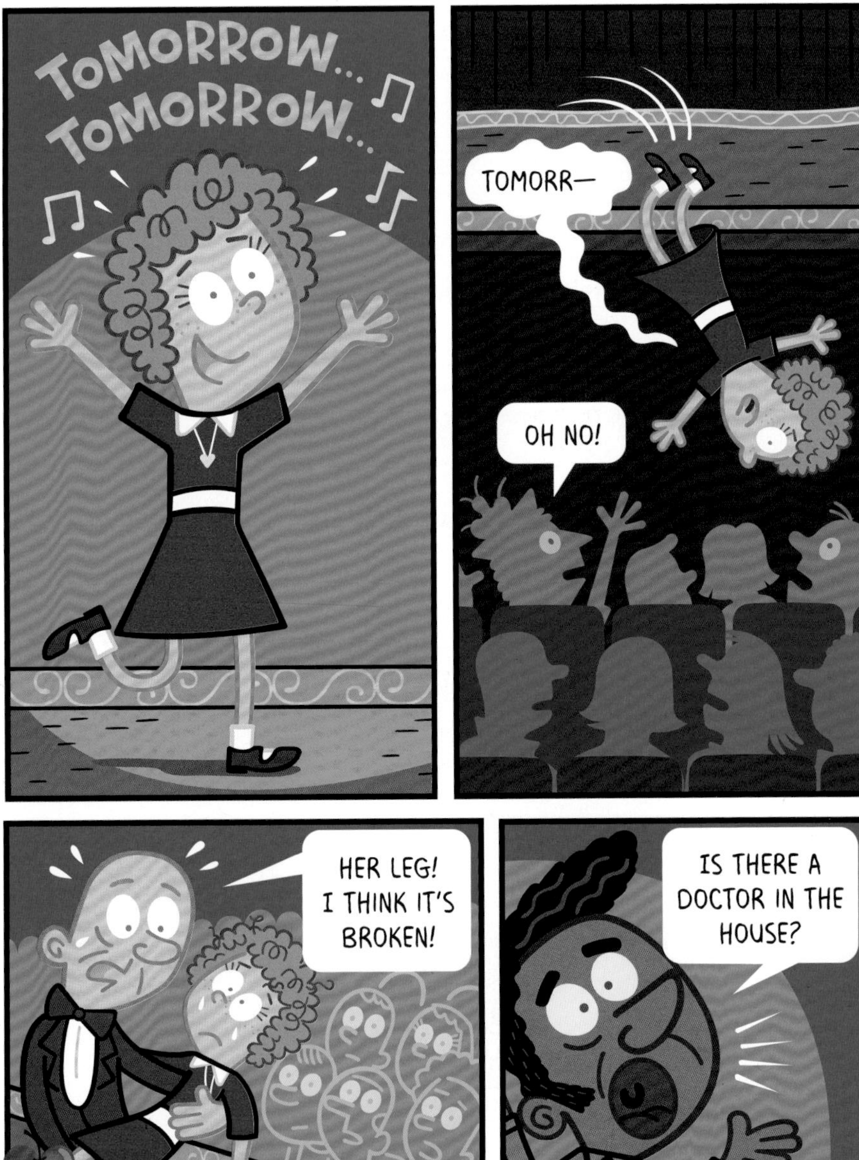
TOMORROW... TOMORROW...
TOMORR—
OH NO!
HER LEG! I THINK IT'S BROKEN!
IS THERE A DOCTOR IN THE HOUSE?

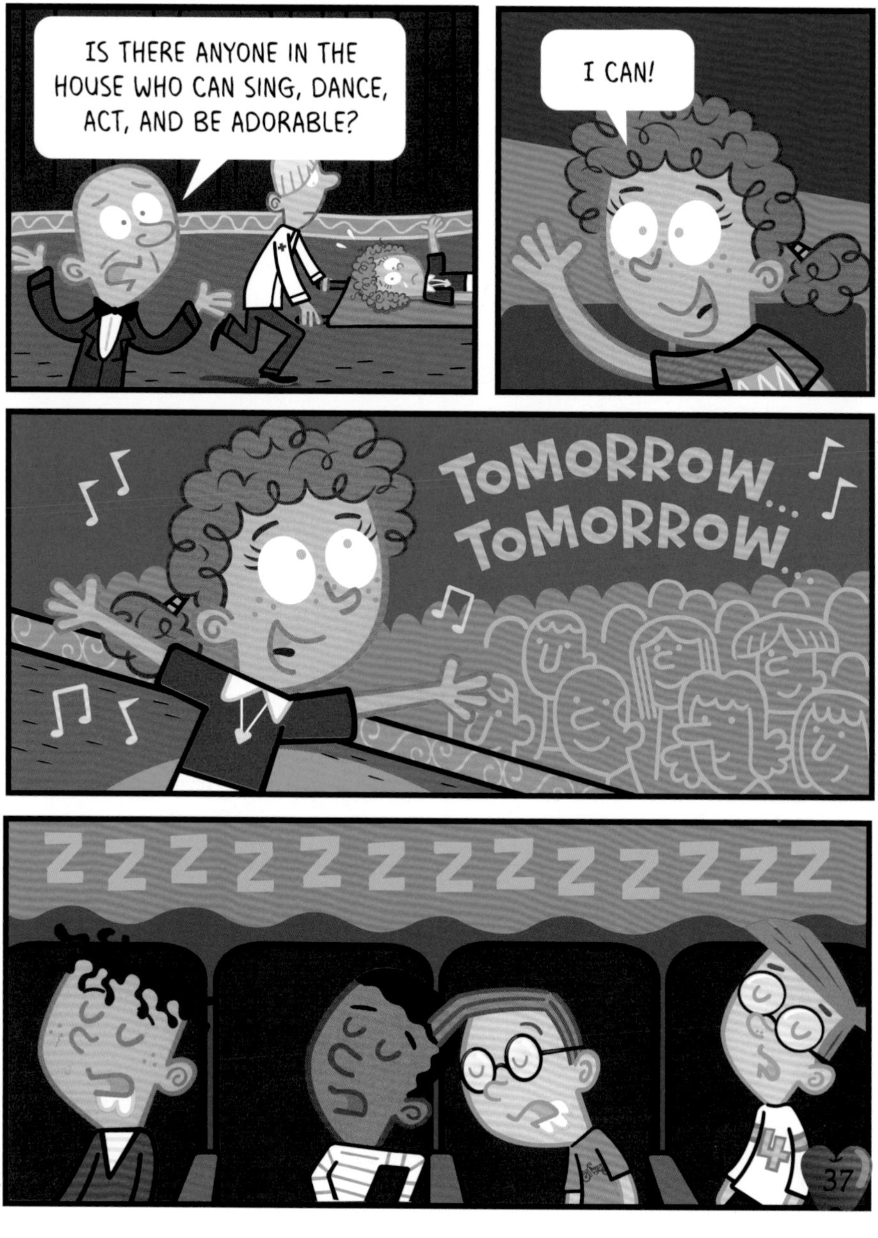
IS THERE ANYONE IN THE HOUSE WHO CAN SING, DANCE, ACT, AND BE ADORABLE?
I CAN!
TOMORROW... TOMORROW...
Z Z Z Z Z Z Z Z Z Z Z Z

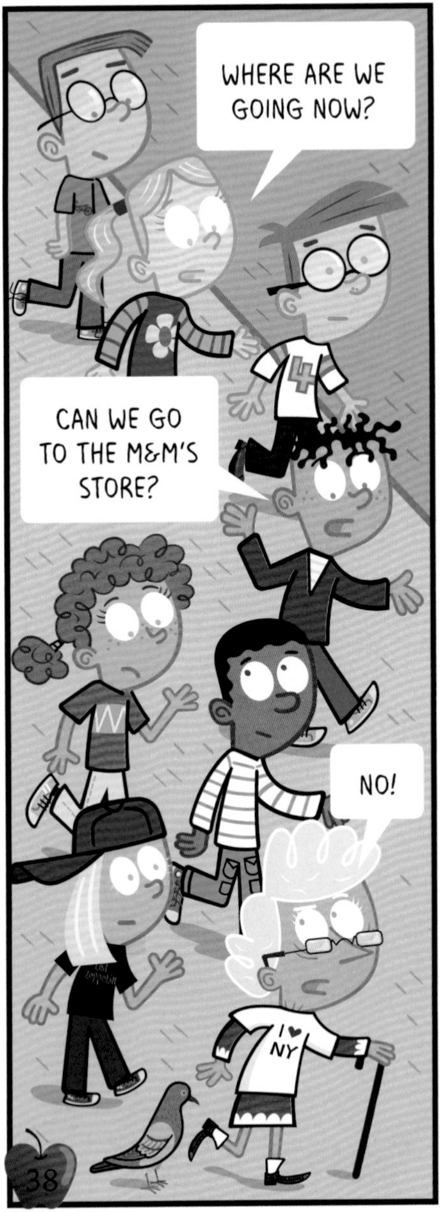
WHERE ARE WE GOING NOW?
CAN WE GO TO THE M&M'S STORE?
NO!
I ♥ NY

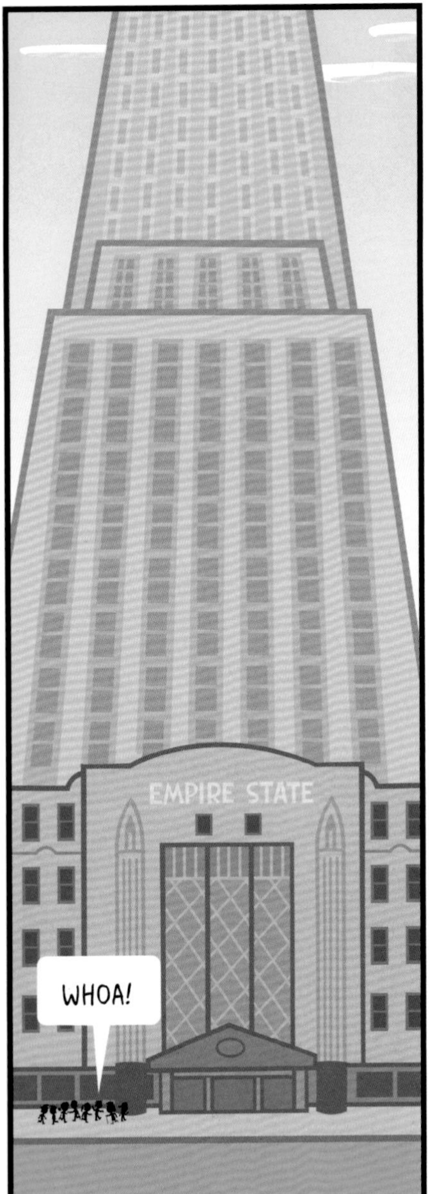
EMPIRE STATE
WHOA!

Weird Stuff about the Empire State Building

IT TOOK JUST 410 DAYS TO BUILD.

IT HAS ITS OWN ZIP CODE: 10118

IT WAS ORIGINALLY GOING TO BE USED AS A BLIMP DOCKING STATION.

THERE'S AN ANNUAL RACE TO RUN UP 1,576 STEPS TO THE 86TH FLOOR.

ON A CLEAR DAY, YOU CAN SEE UP TO 80 MILES FROM THE TOP.

YOU CAN GET MARRIED ON THE 80TH FLOOR.

IN 1986, TWO GUYS PARACHUTED OFF THE 86TH FLOOR OBSERVATION DECK.

BECAUSE OF STATIC ELECTRICITY, COUPLES CAN GET A SHOCK WHILE KISSING AT HIGH LEVELS.

IT WAS THE TALLEST BUILDING IN THE WORLD FOR NEARLY FORTY YEARS.

IT HAS 73 ELEVATORS.

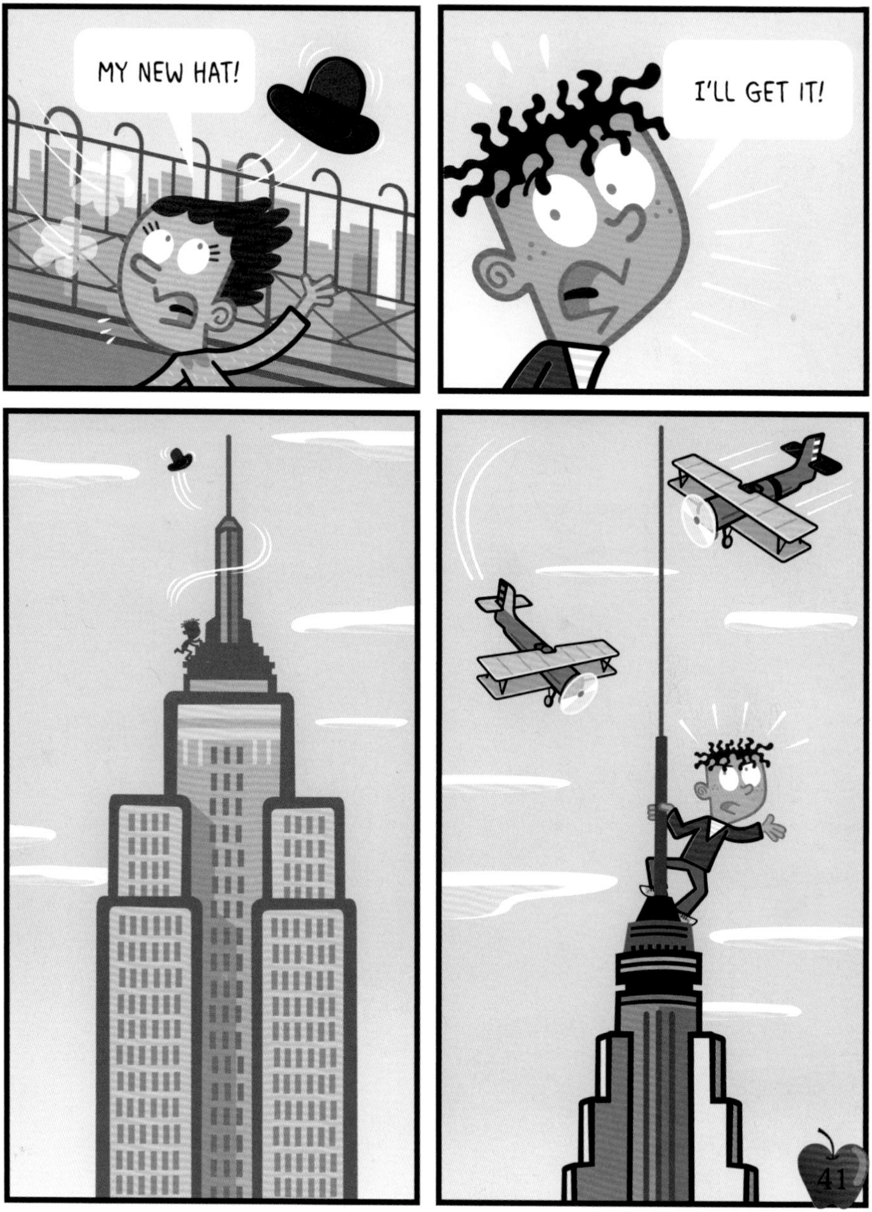
MY NEW HAT!
I'LL GET IT!

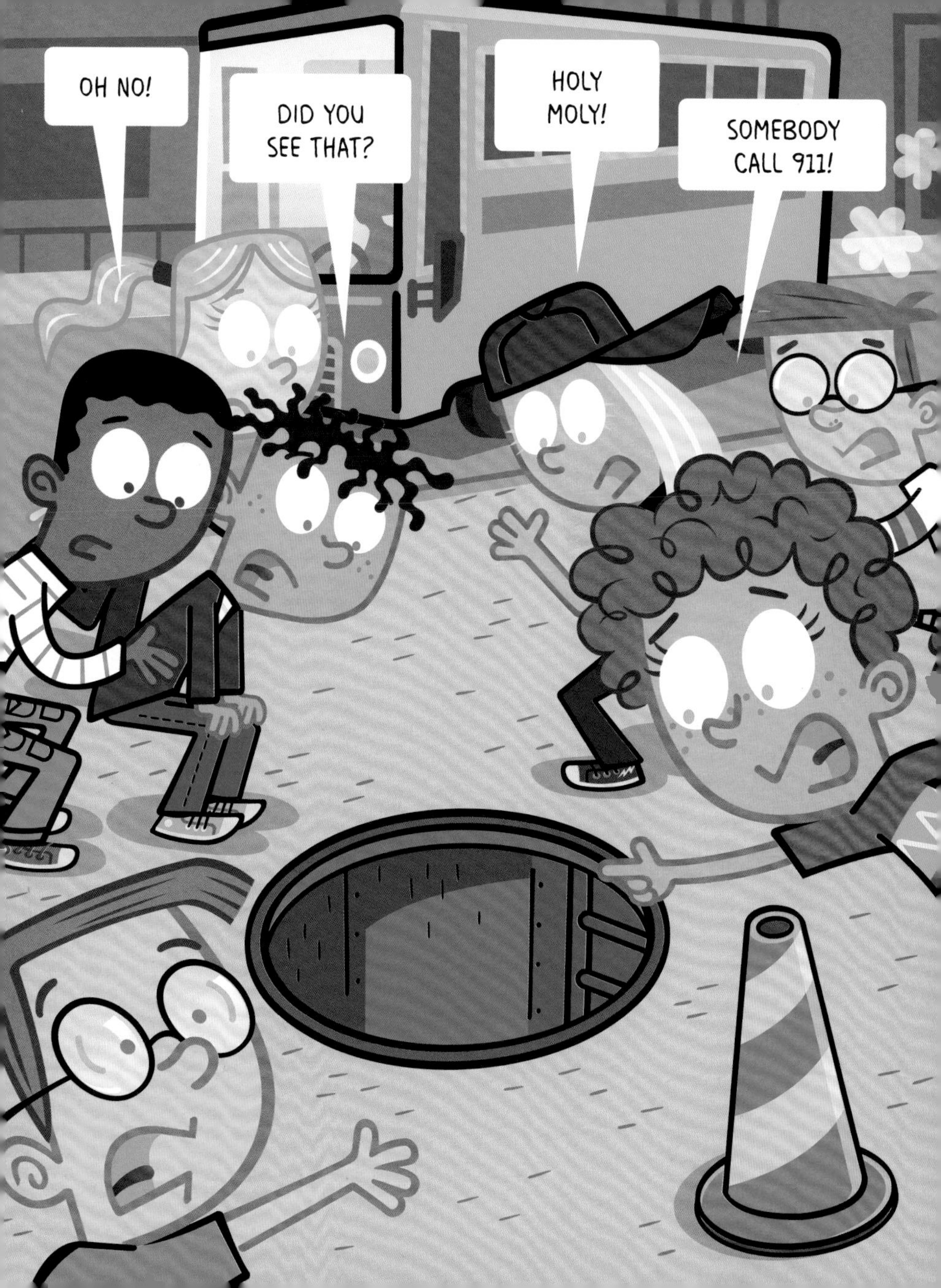
OH NO!
DID YOU SEE THAT?
HOLY MOLY!
SOMEBODY CALL 911!

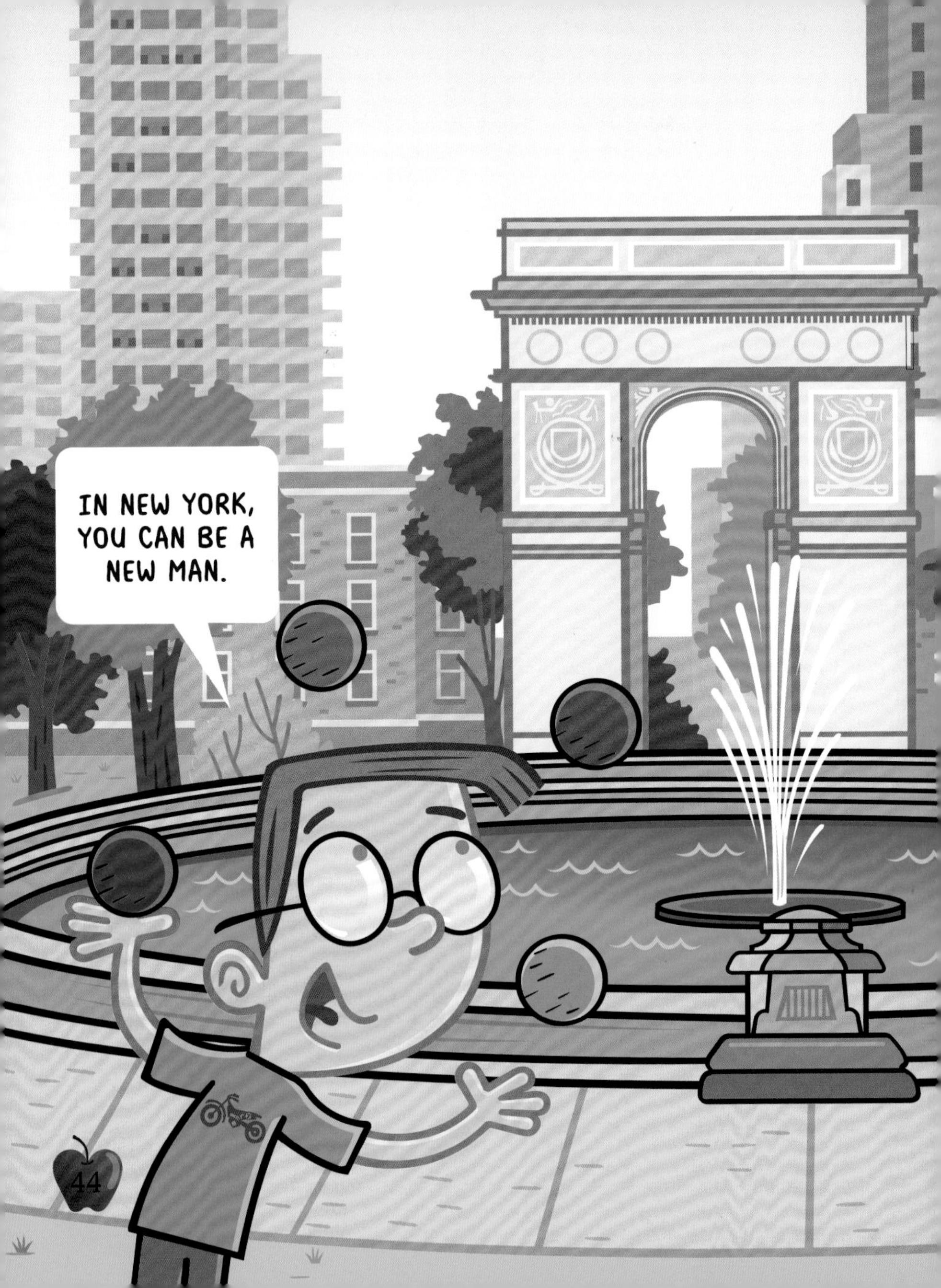
IN NEW YORK, YOU CAN BE A NEW MAN.

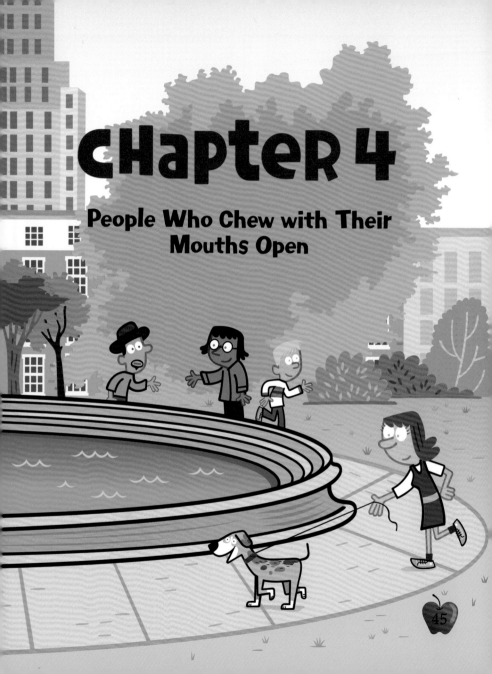

CHAPTER 4

People Who Chew with Their Mouths Open

BREAKING NEWS
THIS IS TAB BATTAN WITH BREAKING NEWS. AN ELDERLY WOMAN HAS FALLEN INTO AN OPEN MANHOLE IN NEW YORK CITY NEAR THE EMPIRE STATE BUILDING. SHE IS BELIEVED TO BE ON TOP OF A MOVING SUBWAY CAR. POLICE AND EMERGENCY RESCUE TEAMS ARE RACING TO THE SCENE. BUT IN THE TOP STORY OF THE DAY, A MEMBER OF THE JARDISHIAN FAMILY BROKE A FINGERNAIL OPENING A JAR OF PEANUT BUTTER. WE WILL STAY ON THIS STORY AND KEEP YOU INFORMED OF FURTHER DEVELOPMENTS.
NEW YORK, 3:45 P.M. EST
LIVE
BNN
NEWS. NEW NEWS. OLD NEWS. REAL NEWS. FAKE NEWS. WE FILL TIME 24/7. SAME NEWS OVER AND OVER AGAIN. WE BRING YOU NEWS EVEN IF NOTHING HAPPENS. IF YOU TURN US OFF, YOU'LL MISS THE NEWS. IF WE DON'T TALK ABOUT IT, IT'S NOT NEWS NEWS NEWS NEWS NEWS NEWS NEWS NEWS NEWS . . .

49

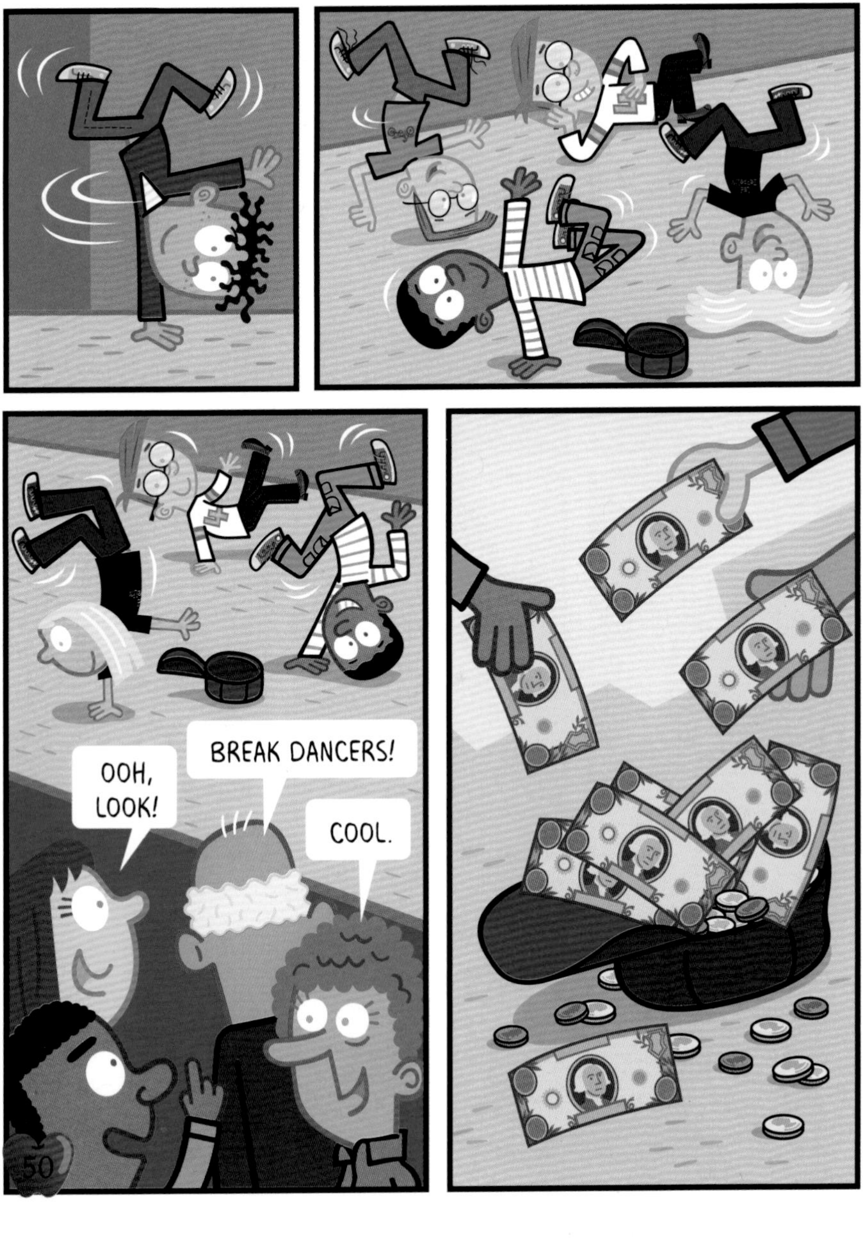
OOH, LOOK!
BREAK DANCERS!
COOL.

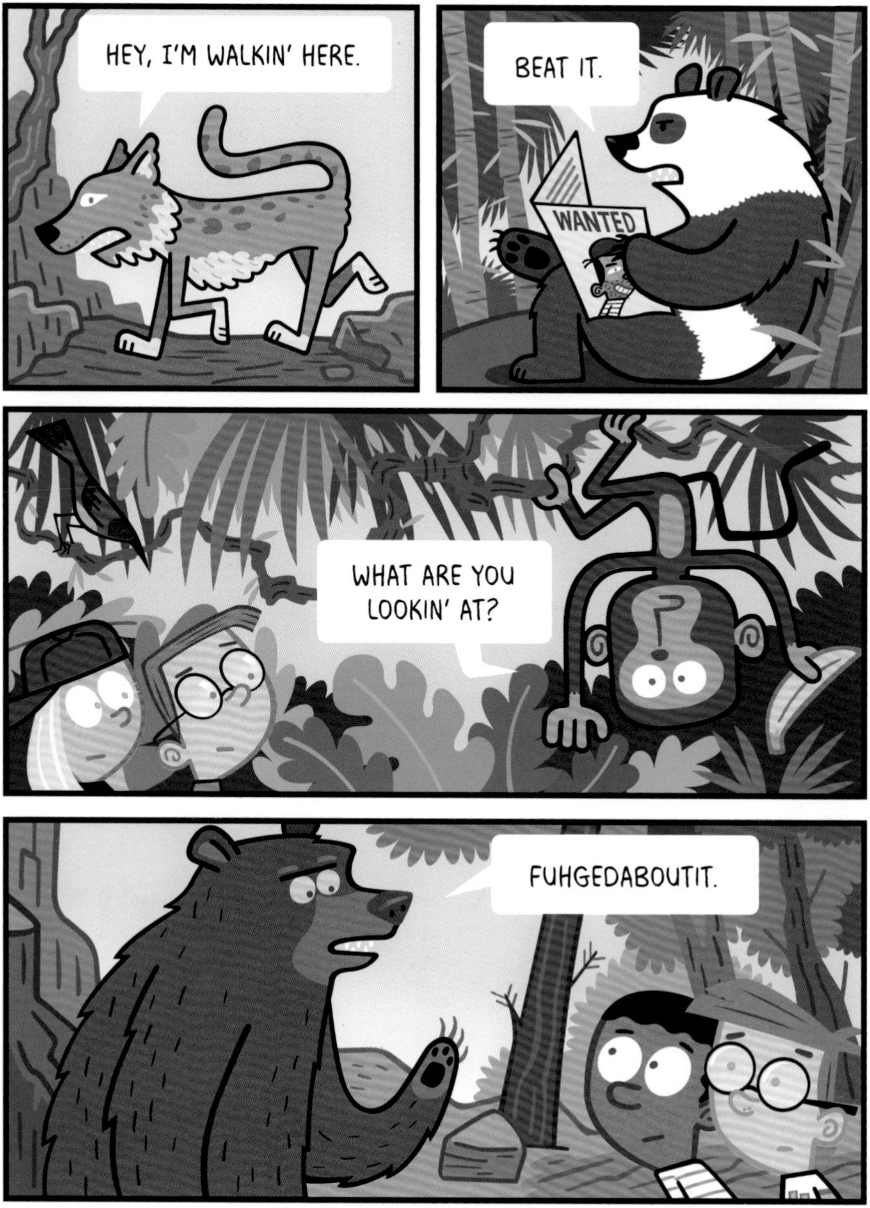
HEY, I'M WALKIN' HERE.
BEAT IT.
WANTED
WHAT ARE YOU LOOKIN' AT?
FUHGEDABOUTIT.

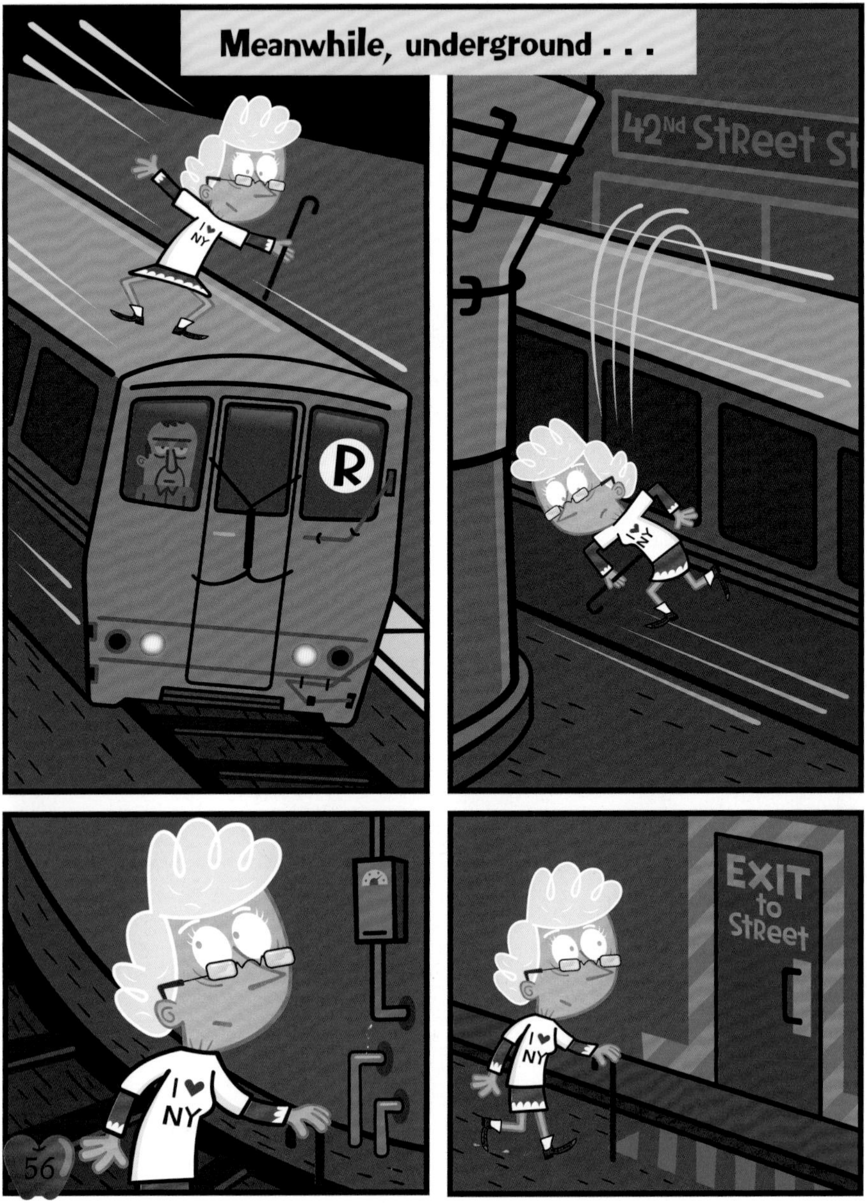
Meanwhile, underground . . .
I ♥ NY
R
42Nd StReet St
I ♥ NY
I ♥ NY
EXIT to StReet
I ♥ NY

Help A.J. Find

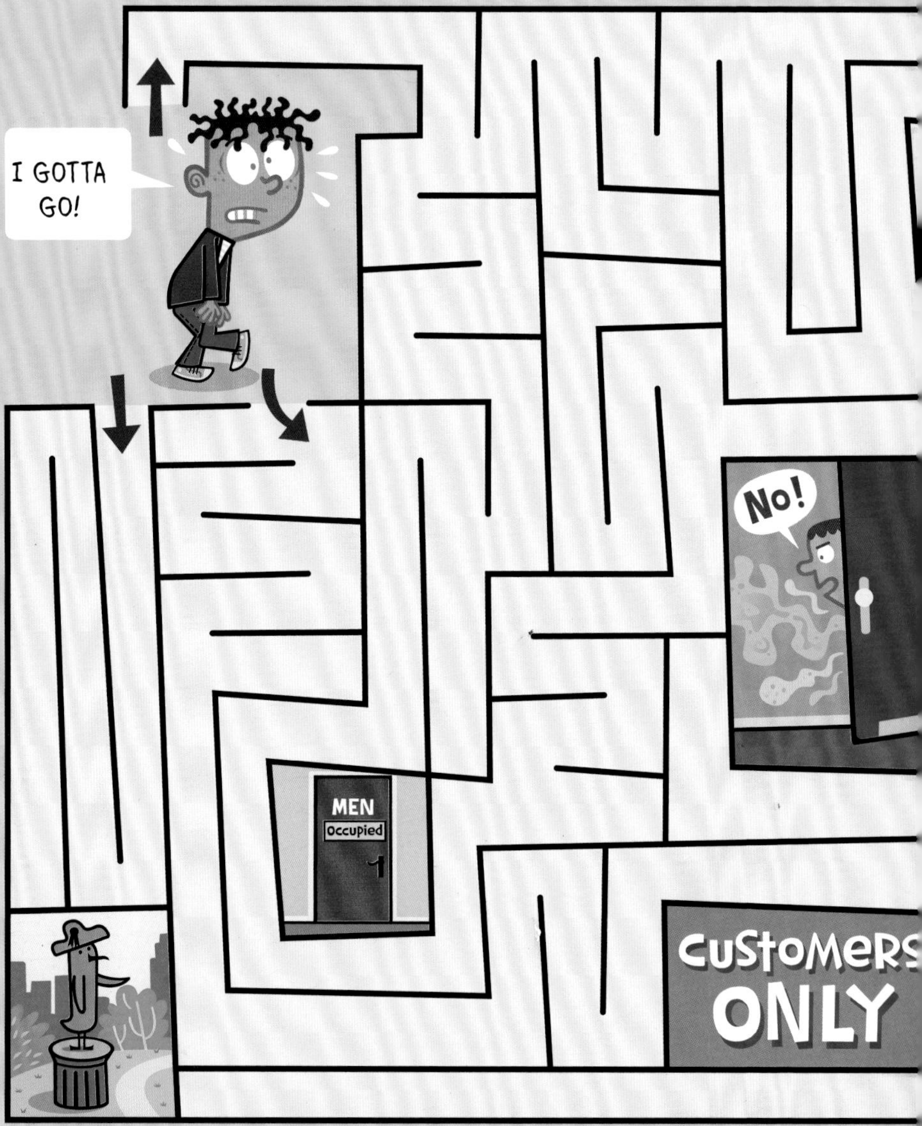
I GOTTA GO!
No!
MEN
Occupied
CUSTOMERS ONLY

63

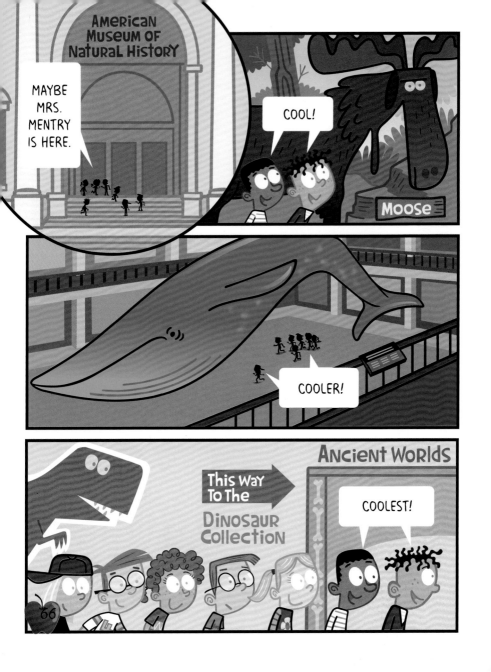

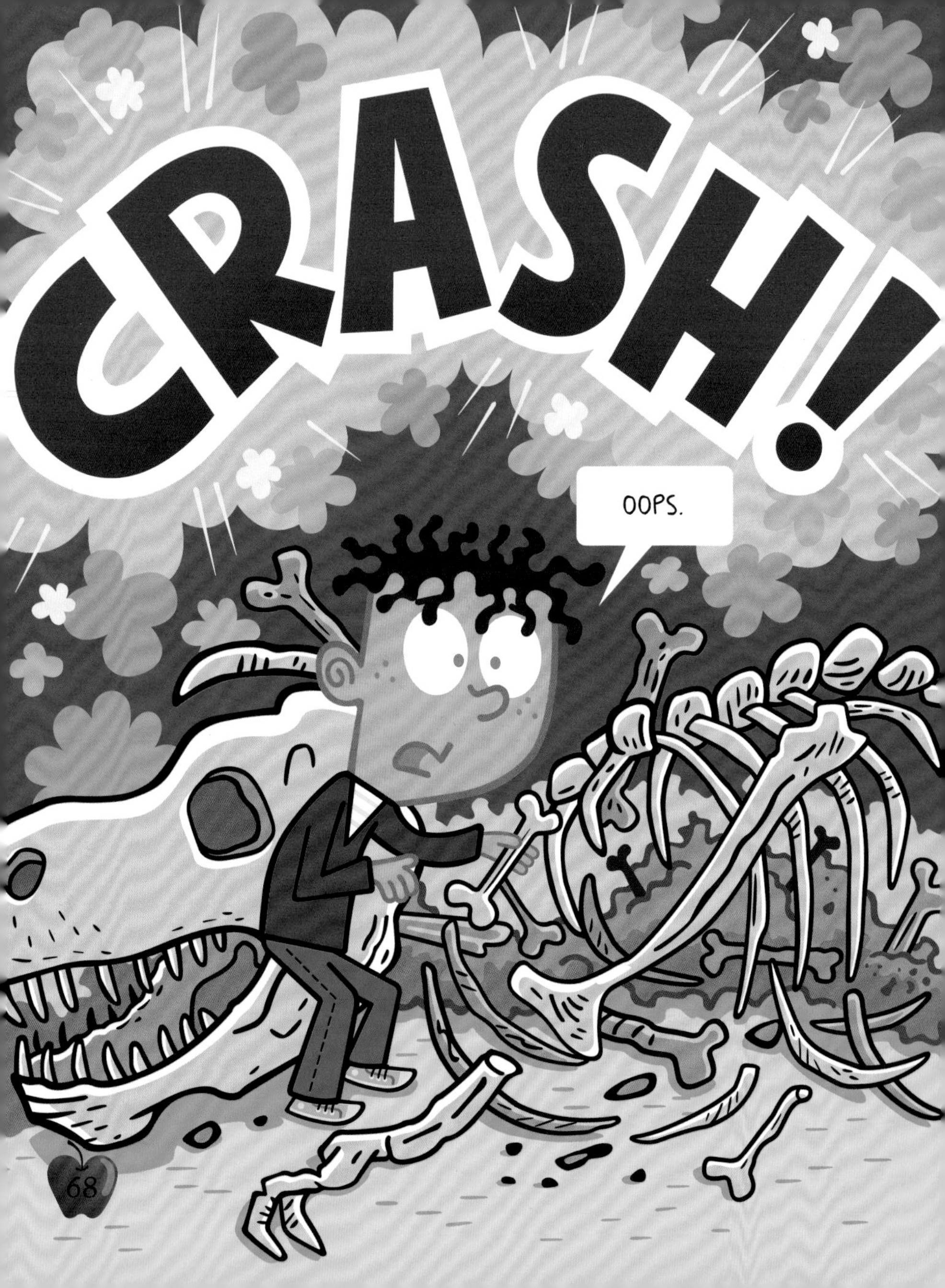
CRASH!!
OOPS.

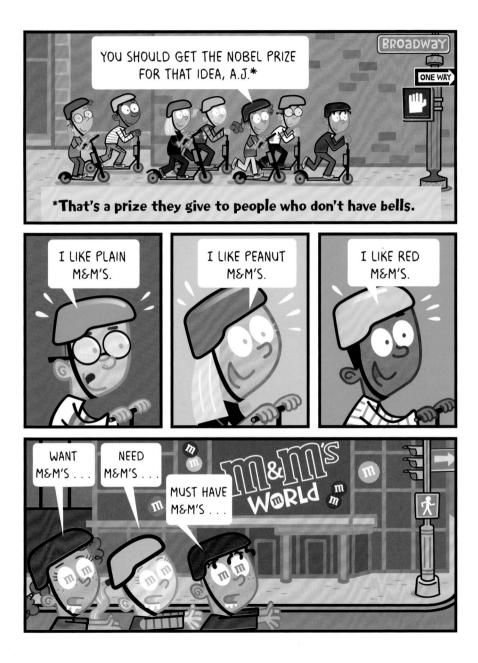

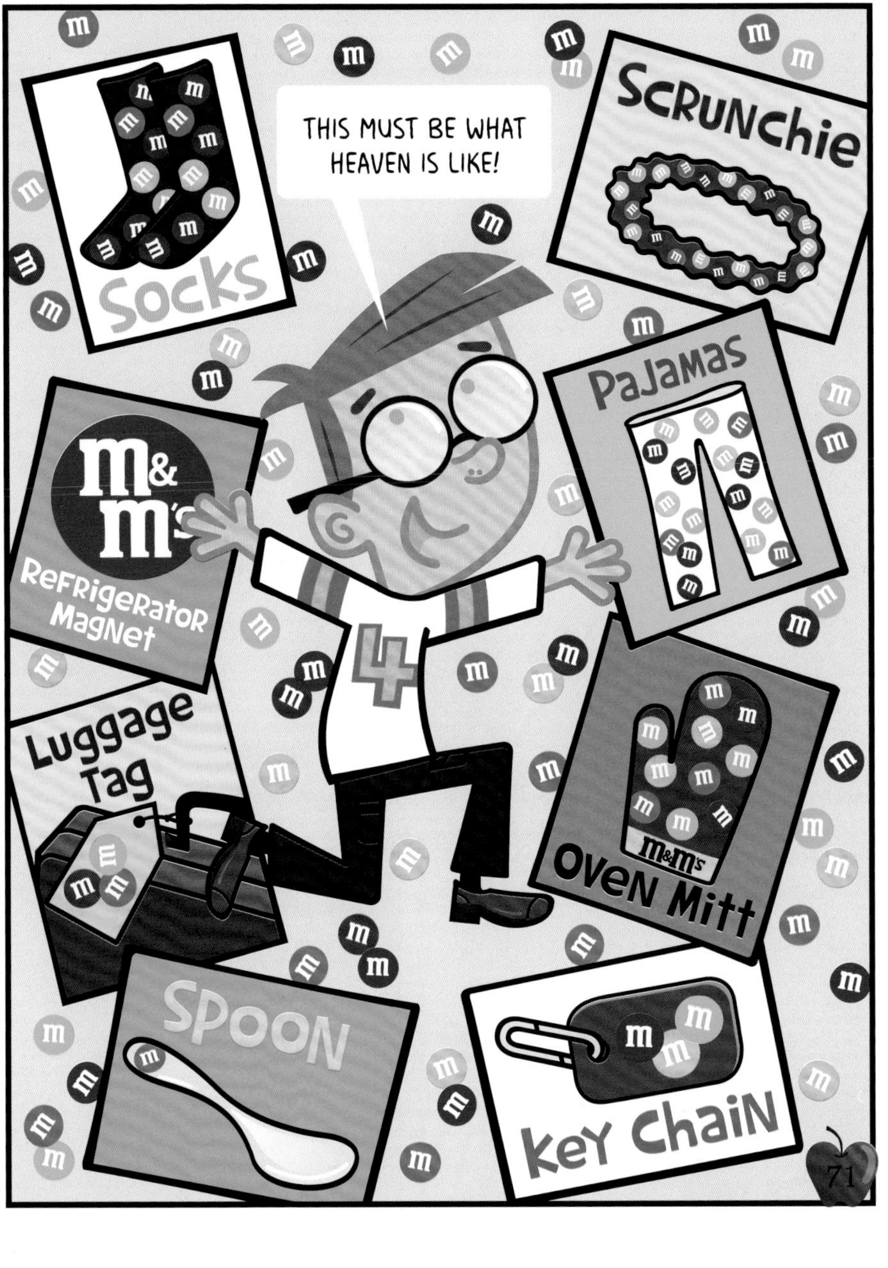
THIS MUST BE WHAT HEAVEN IS LIKE!
Socks
Scrunchie
Pajamas
m&m's
Refrigerator Magnet
Luggage Tag
Oven Mitt
Spoon
Key Chain

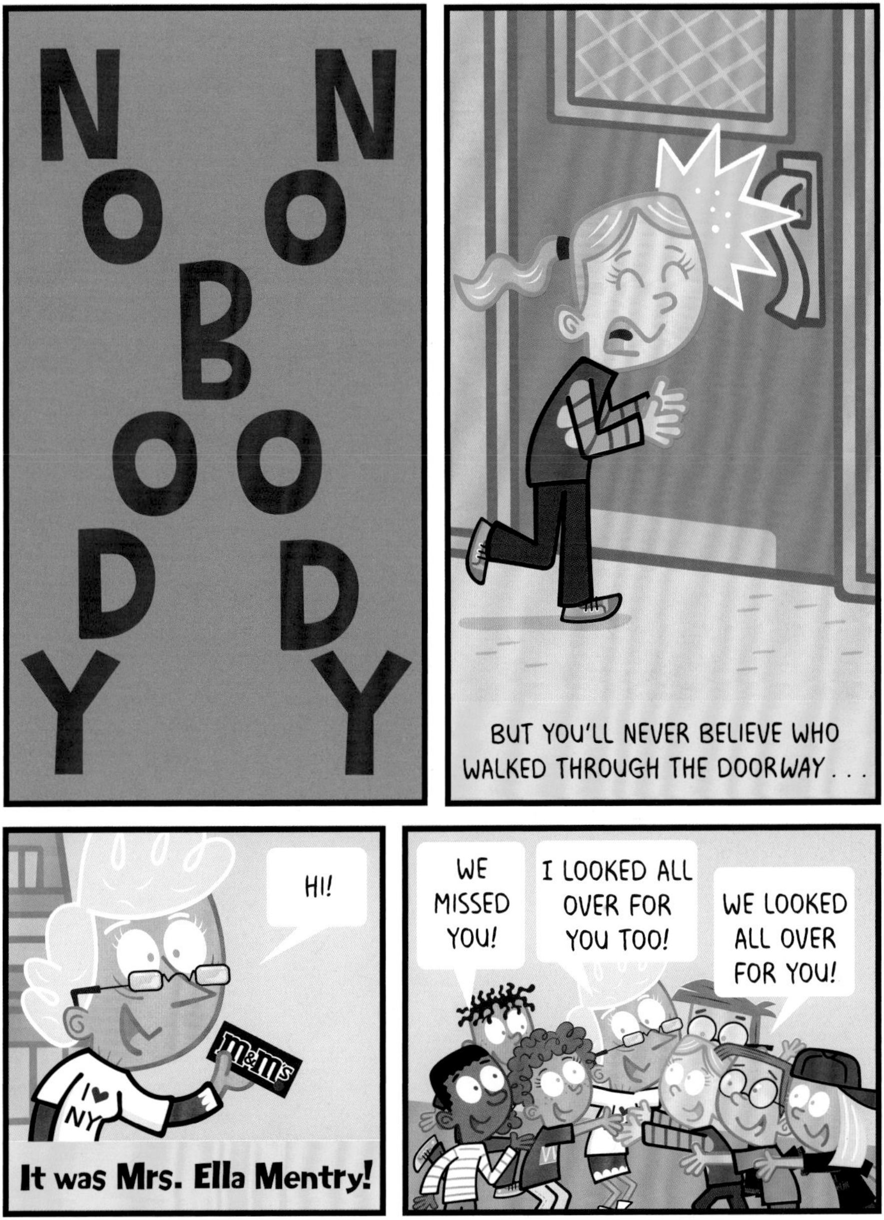
NOBODY NOBODY
BUT YOU'LL NEVER BELIEVE WHO WALKED THROUGH THE DOORWAY . . .
HI!
M&M'S
I ♥ NY
It was Mrs. Ella Mentry!
WE MISSED YOU!
I LOOKED ALL OVER FOR YOU TOO!
WE LOOKED ALL OVER FOR YOU!

74

CHAPTER 5

People Who Talk on Their Cell Phones Loudly in Public. People Who Don't Pick Up Their Dog's Poop. Loud Chewers. Litterbugs. People Who Put Their Recyclables in with the Regular Trash. People Who Stand and Talk to Each Other in the Middle of a Busy Sidewalk.

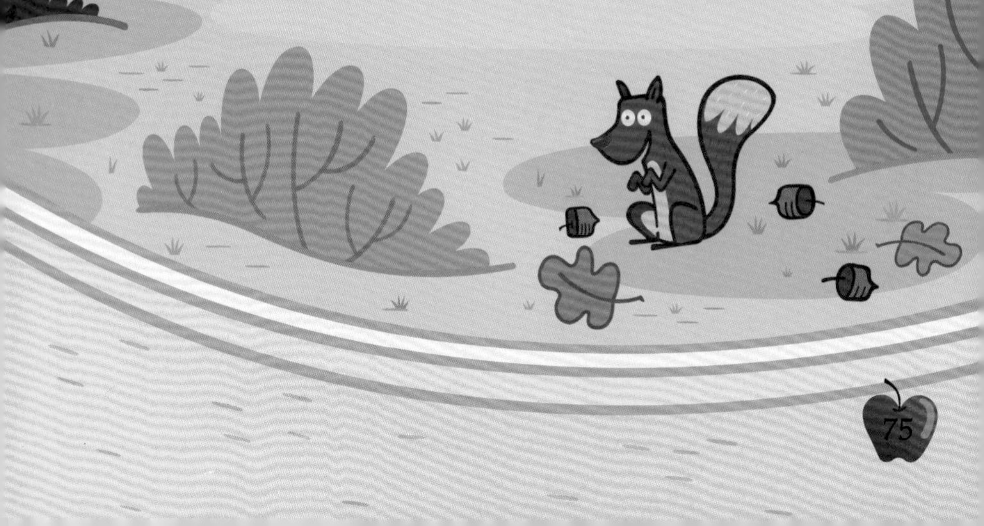

THAT'S WHEN THE WEIRDEST THING IN THE HISTORY OF THE WORLD HAPPENED!

76

77

BREAKING NEWS
NEWS NEWS NEWS NEWS NEWS NEWS NEWS NEWS NEWS NEWS
I NEED A DAY OFF NEWS SOMEBODY GET ME OUTTA HERE

THIS IS TAB BATTAN WITH BREAKING NEWS. IN AN AMAZING TURN OF EVENTS, THE PRICELESS *THE STARRY NIGHT* PAINTING BY VINCENT VAN GOGH HAS BEEN FOUND HANGING IN A TIMES SQUARE SOUVENIR SHOP BY THE OLD LADY WHO FELL INTO AN OPEN MANHOLE AND A GROUP OF OBNOXIOUS KIDS WHO HAD BEEN MISSING SINCE YESTERDAY. THE THIEF WHO STOLE THE MASTERPIECE HAS BEEN CAPTURED. SADLY, THE ANIMALS THAT ESCAPED FROM THE CENTRAL PARK ZOO YESTERDAY HAVE NOT BEEN FOUND. BUT THE TOP STORY OF THE DAY CONCERNS THE JARDISHIAN FAMILY . . .

TOP STORY

THE STARRY NIGHT FOUND!

MISSING KIDS CATCH CROOK!

OLD LADY IS OKAY!

ZOO ANIIMALS STILL MISSING!

LIVE

BNN

4/7 UGH NEWS
WS NEWS . . .